P9-CLW-699

At the edge
of the world

At the Edge of the World

Magical Stories of Ireland

Illustrated with Photographs by

JOHN LOWINGS

HENRY HOLT AND COMPANY

NEW YORK

Henry Holt and Company, Inc.
Publishers since 1866
115 West 18th Street
New York, New York 10011

Henry Holt ® is a registered trademark of
Henry Holt and Company, Inc.
Copyright © 1998 by John Lowings
All rights reserved.

Owing to limitations of space, sources for previously
published materials may be found on page 173–74.

Library of Congress Cataloging-in-Publication Data
At the edge of the world : magical stories of Ireland /
illustrated with photographs by John Lowings.
p.   cm.
Includes bibliographical references (p.   ).
ISBN 0-8050-5400-6 (hb : alk. paper)
1. Fantastic fiction, English—Irish authors.
2. Tales—Ireland—Adaptations.
3. Mythology, Celtic—Fiction. 4. Folklore—Ireland—Fiction.
5. Supernatural—Fiction. 6. Fairy tales—Ireland.
I. Lowings, John.
PR8876.5.F35A92   1998   97-39616
823'.08766089415—dc21   CIP

Henry Holt books are available for special promotions and premiums.
For details contact: Director, Special Markets.

First Edition 1998

Designed by Lucy Albanese

All photographs were taken in County Mayo.

Printed in the United States of America
All first editions are printed on acid-free paper. ∞
1   3   5   7   9   10 8   6   4   2

FOR RORY

CONTENTS

~

$\mathcal{A}$CKNOWLEDGEMENTS

This is my first book, and in the course of producing it I have become very aware that, finally, a book is the synthesis of many people's contributions, without which this one would either never have seen the light of day, or would have, in a much poorer form. I am extremely grateful to the following people for their kindness, help, and guidance at various stages of what has been a bit of an odyssey for me. My heartfelt thanks go to the McConnell family of the Shraugh in Mayo for their warm welcome and hot suppers, which cast a rosy glow over many chilly winter evenings; to Mark and Gaynor Ranshaw for taking such a pleasant unexpected interest in the pictures and giving them their first showing; to Alivia Rose and all my Thursday-evening colleagues for their wonderful support when most needed; to my brother Luke for taking the project so thoroughly in hand at a vital stage; to Sheree Bykofsky for introducing it to the wider world; and to Theresa Burns, Ray Roberts, and everyone involved in producing the book so professionally at Henry Holt.

Most of all though I would like to thank my wife, Maggie for being such a wholehearted companion on this journey and for always knowing it would end in the right place.

$\mathcal{I}$NTRODUCTION

$\mathcal{O}$ne hundred and sixty years ago there is no electric light. When the sun goes down it becomes dark outside. Inside, the unsteady glow from oil lamp and turf fire is gentle and welcoming but hardly bright enough to read by. Shadows accumulate in the corners of the smallest cabin. Outside there is only darkness—and the wind, whose whispers or howls mask other sounds. On still nights there is silence. Moonlight is deliciously silver but throws absolute shadows. When it is cloudy, there is no light at all. The darkness is a blank space, in which creatures from the twilight corners of our minds can grow, unfettered by the sharp focus of day.

A cabin encloses a family. Inside, there is a rich soup of relationships. Three generations of experiences under the same small roof. When the door closes against the dark, there is the whole evening to while away. For a sociable and imaginative people, time does not hang heavy. Without television or radio to drip-feed them entertainment, the Irish tell each other stories. The cabin is an engine for ideas, and over hundreds of years, in the countless thousands of households throughout the length and breadth of Ireland, an opulent wealth of tales is amassed.

In most townlands there was at least one "visiting-house"; usually the home of a particularly talented musician or storyteller, whose door was always open to the neighbours to come and share in the enjoyment of the evening. On most evenings friends would gather in the warm glow of the fire, and with the door shut against the night they would retell ancient stories or invent their own. The great, old stories were communicated down the generations with extraordinary accuracy for centuries. At the same time, their themes became interwoven with people's own experiences, and the more intimate folktales developed.

The Celts are said to have originated in the Middle East, and they slowly migrated westward, finally being driven to the western seaboard of Europe. The great themes of their tales can be found in recognizable forms wherever they lived throughout Europe. In ancient times, the Welsh, Scots, and Irish Celts, though frequently warring, shared a culture, in which the stories played a vital part. Some were written down by ecclesiastical scribes, but the vast majority were passed down by word of mouth. As long as Celtic society remained vibrant this cultural treasure was kept alive.

By the early part of the nineteenth century, though, the Celts in Ireland had been displaced from the best agricultural land by their English rulers. For reasons which are still unclear, the late eighteenth and early nineteenth centuries had seen an unprecedented population explosion, until at the start of the 1840s, Ireland was, according to Disraeli, more densely populated than anywhere else in Europe. The population was almost exclusively rural, and, through the succeeding generations, land had been divided, and subdivided, to such a degree that, in a great many cases, families were having to subsist on less than half an acre of arable ground. The density of population was such that the most marginal land was pressed into use—land that, today, would be regarded as quite unsuitable for cultivation. The only crop that would grow with sufficient abundance to support so many people was the potato.

So, the Irish, taxed by their English landlords in such a way as to render improvement of holdings self-defeating, and forced onto the worst land, whilst the best was used to raise grain, meat, and dairy produce—which was then exported to England and the colonies—lived almost exclusively on the potato. Surprisingly, the people were, on the whole, fit and healthy. If eaten in sufficient quantities, the potato will support life and health. Quantities, though, had to be large—a working man needed twelve pounds of potatoes a day! Cultivation was by the spade, in raised ridges of soil—an extremely effective method, much derided in England at the time. These distinctive ridges are still visible throughout the west of Ireland, climbing out of valleys into the moorland above and, in remote places, pushing down to the very edge of the sea. That they were dubbed "lazy beds" by English observers is, in itself, indicative of the prevailing attitude towards the native Irish.

One hundred and sixty years ago there were teeming millions of Irish peasant farmers, living on rented land, in little rural settlements, reaching into the most remote and inhospitable parts of the country. In spite—or perhaps because—of their poverty, homeless, travelling people were generally assured of a place to sleep for the night and a bite for supper, by simply knocking at a cabin door. They were welcomed in and shared the fare of the family for the night. Sustained by their boundless sociability and their rich cultural heritage, they were a cheerful and warmhearted people.

However, with such a dependance on one foodstuff, it was only a matter of time before they were visited by a disaster. In 1845 there was a partial failure of the potato crop, from what we now know as blight, resulting in severe hardship and some starvation for the poorest farmers. In 1846 and 1847 the crop was utterly destroyed. From being a rich, particularly promising crop, the fields of lush green growth were reduced—overnight—to blackened, stinking mush. Much of the population of Ireland was left with nothing to eat. Millions starved and died of typhus and cholera in scenes of grotesque degradation. Millions more left what now seemed to them to be a doomed country. Whole communities disappeared all over Ireland. The overwhelming sense of apocalypse that overtook the country at that time is hard for modern Western people to imagine.

Today, the richness and vibrancy of traditional Irish culture is rightly acknowledged all over the world, but in the nineteenth century it was a very different picture. The English had dominated and exploited Ireland politically, and reviled the Irish culturally, for so long that, even in Ireland, the middle and upper classes (where they existed) had come to see anything to do with the native Irish as being beneath contempt. English and Anglo-Irish overlords had developed fiendish schemes to try to stamp out the use of Gaelic as the language of the Celts. Educated people strove to distance themselves from Irishness and struggled towards an ideal of English upper-class manners and culture. The hoard of stories was either completely unknown to the educated classes or was regarded with derision. The disaster that overwhelmed Ireland after 1845 rocked all levels of Irish society to their foundations, but its effects were most bitterly felt by the poor peasant farmers—the people to whom these stories formed an integral part of their everyday lives. With the destruction of communities and loss of confidence in their own culture that followed the famine, the use of the stories began to decline. In England the process of industrialization had already made huge inroads into rural traditions. In Scotland the Highland Clearances had similarly undermined traditional culture. On the mainland, folklorists, attempting to prevent these cultural jewels from being lost forever, had already begun to "collect" stories and write them down, but for the reasons I have pointed out, hardly any attempts had been made to write down Irish stories.

Thomas Crofton Croker—a Scots antiquarian—was the first to make literature out of the folktales. He published the delightful *Fairy Legends and Traditions of the South of Ireland* (anonymously) in three parts from 1825–28. It is revealing that, in spite of the patronage of Lady Chatterton, he did not feel safe to publish under his own name until much later. We must assume that he felt the need to wait and see how his material would be received. Later writers have taken exception to Croker's undoubted manipulation of the stories; he made no attempt to adhere to the original language of the tellers, and he probably added and removed parts to make them more accessible to his educated audience. To appreciate his work, though, we have to remember the

cultural climate in which it was produced. Croker broke the ground for later writers.

Working in the latter part of the nineteenth century Patrick Kennedy was a bookseller in Dublin. His stories came from the southeast of Ireland—mainly from County Wexford—and were collected from English-speaking country folk. Whilst Kennedy endeavored to reproduce the language of the teller as far as possible, in places transcribing a tale word for word, some commentators have observed that the very Anglicization of the material that makes it work so well for an English-speaking audience also makes his tales mere shadows of those told in the original Gaelic. Later folklorists have suggested that he altered the material in order to make it more commercially viable. According to Douglas Hyde, "We cannot be sure how much belongs to Kennedy the bookseller, and how much to the Wexford peasant."

The question of how to record and present the stories has always been vexing—Anglicization being inevitably associated with imperialism. William Carleton—himself from a peasant background—wrote his stories from childhood memories. He was a great raconteur and originally produced them for the amusement of his friends. Thus, they are a long way removed, in language and form, from the original material. Furthermore, Carleton's usual style of writing, in which a particularly droll Irish brogue is reproduced phonetically, is more or less insufferable in a modern context. Thankfully, some of his work was rather more respectful; the piece I have used here is particularly worthwhile.

Lady Wilde (mother of Oscar) was a member of the landed upper class and was instrumental in igniting the "Celtic Revival"—that renaissance of Irish culture that developed around such figures as W. B. Yeats, J. M. Synge, and Lady Gregory. In Yeats's words, "The best book since Croker is Lady Wilde's 'Ancient Legends.' The humour has all given way to pathos and tenderness. We have here the innermost heart of the Celt in the moments he has grown to love through years of persecution, when, cushioning himself about with dreams, and hearing fairy-songs in the twilight, he ponders on the soul and on the dead." Not being "of the people" though, and being ignorant of Irish,

Lady Wilde was guilty of some rather colourful inaccuracies, such as her assertion that peasants wished each other good luck with, "The blessing of Bel and the blessing of Samhain [the sun and the moon] be with you." This was, in fact, completely unheard of. Personally, I forgive her her romanticizations for the beauty of her stories.

Dr. P. W. Joyce was very much alive to the issues of translation and presentation. He resented the way in which some writers had reduced the characters in the old tales to being, "mere stage Irish." On this subject: "There is none of this silly and odious vulgarity in the originals of these fine old tales, which are high and dignified in tone and feeling—quite as much so as the old romantic tales of Greece and Rome." Joyce worked from those originals, some having been made as long ago as A.D. 1100, and being themselves copies of still older works. His translations were designed to be as close as he could manage to the way in which, he imagined, the professional storytellers of that time *would* have told them if they had used English instead of Gaelic. So whilst he remained faithful to the content and sequence of events in the originals, the flavour of the language is nothing like the Irish.

Joseph Jacobs's work was published at the end of the nineteenth century. He was a sensitive and knowledgeable folklorist whose books of fairy stories were edited from material collected by others. We are indebted to these folklorists for tracing the connecting threads between stories of different nations and hence showing us how peoples and their cultures have travelled. However, they "collected" their stories—and there is a negative connotation to the word in this context. They saw their work as a science, and, in their zeal to erase the subjective, there was a tendency amongst them to translate the stories overliterally. Though not necessarily in itself a fault, this can make wonderful material just about unreadable. When a folklorist transcribed a story word for word he did not also transcribe the atmosphere in which the story was told. He did not transcribe the rain on the window, the press of people in the warm room, each individual's prior knowledge of the story, or their foreboding at the prospect of the dark journey home at the end of the evening. All these things—along with the subtle inflections of voice, the timing of the run of a sentence, or the tense pauses for anticipation—crucially affect the way a story is heard and understood. If a story is reproduced word for word, its meaning to a reader from a different culture is impenetrable. The folklorist's fidelity to the language of the original consigns the material to the library vaults.

To make the stories work for a nonscholarly audience, the writer has to take the responsibility of reinterpreting them for the medium of print, whilst, hopefully, remaining faithful to the timbre and flavour of the original. Croker understood this but erred towards the flippant; Lady Wilde understood but erred towards the romantic. Many people feel that the best translations are those by Dr. Douglas Hyde. Whilst the language of Dr. Hyde's stories is readily accessible to the modern ear, he manages to retain something of the astringent vigour of the original Irish. He was a native Irish speaker, who saw the preservation of the stories told by ordinary people as a part of the process of validating a culture that the English had tried to squeeze out of existence. He felt it was vital that the feel of the original language be communicated as closely as possible in order for the cultural value of the stories to be realized. It should be no surprise that he went on to become the first president of the Irish Republic.

Lady Gregory, however, was also from the landed upper classes. She spent her life on the family's estate of Coole Park in County Galway and, in her teens, became aware that the family's tenants—who spoke Irish—were party to a wealth of knowledge and experience from which English speakers were excluded. She and her mother taught themselves Irish and became fluent. Coole Park became the home of the Celtic Revival, and she established the Abbey Theatre there. For many years she collected stories from her tenants and Irish-speaking peasants further afield. Her major work of folklore— *Visions and Beliefs in the West of Ireland*—was published in 1920, but it is largely overlooked in anthologies of folktales. It comprises short snippets of individuals' own experiences retold as accurately as she could remember (not having access to a tape recorder at the time!), and so does not work as entertainment. In this, she was a regular folklorist, but her work has such warmth and respect about it that it demands to be included here. I have edited a piece from the "Sea Stories" section of *Visions and Beliefs* to give a flavour. There is lots more for the interested reader.

"The People of the Sea" is taken from the book of the same name by David Thomson, about his search for the silkies. Written in the early 1950s it is fascinating to see that the ancient tales were, even then, still alive in the remotest reaches of the west. The centuries between the birth of the story and the present moment seem to shrink to nothing.

Whilst photographing driftwood on the beach at Carrowniskey, I met a farmer who had come to cut up my piece of trawler for firewood. In answer to his question I told him I was illustrating a story about a young woman whose lover—who she is about to marry—is drowned, along with all the guests for the wedding, and that, brokenhearted, she too dies. "That sounds like a good Irish tale," said he with a slightly embarrassed laugh. I have not chosen these tales to be safe, lightweight entertainment, though some are closer to the pretty, nursery stories with which we are all familiar than others. I have chosen them because they touch on the primeval fears and fascinations that, even now, flood up from within us to fill the darkness outside. Who has not, at some point in his life, been aware—with a crawling sensation in the small of the back—of the Pooka about to leap on him from behind? Who has not dreamt—like Oisin—of a land where all is beauty and pleasure without pain, only to force himself, with a grim sense of adult responsibility, to acknowledge prosaic reality? This is not a work of scholarship and thus does not have to be representative of the broad sweep of Irish stories. It is the personal choice of a lifelong city-dweller, all too conscious that, in an entirely man-made environment, our sense of the awe and mystery of life has given way to a sort of neurotic narcissism. Rational empiricism—our modern deity—has sought to replace ignorance and superstition with a kind of knowledge, but at the same time it has stripped away much of the wonder from the world and has replaced it with multiple, fractured images of ourselves.

The people that told and heard these stories had a sense that the world is shared with beings other than ourselves. Their response to the landscape in which they lived was different from ours. To us, a landscape is primarily an aesthetic experience. To them, it was, firstly, life and death, in that they ate what they grew themselves on the land. But it also teemed with ghosts and the "Good People." In the words of Lady Gregory, "The *Sidhe* [pronounced *Shee*] cannot make themselves visible to all. They are shape-changers; they can grow small or grow large, they can take what shape they choose; they appear as men or women wearing clothes of many colours, of today or of some old forgotten fashion, or they are seen as bird or beast, or as a barrel or as a flock of wool. They go by us in a cloud of dust; they are as many as the blades of grass." There was a story attached to almost every element of the landscape. As we gaze at one of the thousands of little lakes in the west we may admire the grace of the rushes, rippled by the breeze, but the peasants knew that the rush heads were burnt red by the malign eye of Balor Beimeann as he rampaged throughout the country murdering the natives. To us, the innumerable "fairy forts," clustering thickly along the western seaboard, are evidence of an ancient society's need to defend itself. But the peasants knew that the *Sidhe*, who still, at that time, inhabited the green mounds, were merciless in their punishment of those farmers who, in their arrogance, presumed to interfere with those unprepossessing earthworks. We look at the landscape, but the farmers of ages past were immersed in it.

The *Sidhe* held on, in the west, for longer than concerned observers in the nineteenth century would have believed possible. They had not been seriously discomfited by the invasion of Christianity into the popular mind, though they did have to retreat underground a little deeper. Indeed, the early Christians, acknowledging the resilience of the ancient faith, were obliged to borrow its stories and insert saints to replace heroes. The English strove to control the unruly populace by strangling the language that carried the knowledge of the *Sidhe*, and partly succeeded. A great many stories managed the jump into the English language, though, and pressed on vigorously until the famine and resulting social upheavals blew the Irish all over the globe and evaporated their confidence in their own culture. W. B. Yeats, Lady Gregory, and the rest of the Celtic Revival resuscitated the *Sidhe,* and the folklorists ensured that knowledge of them was not entirely lost. As long as the tradition of "visiting-houses" survived, the *Sidhe* hung on in Ireland, however furtively, but the phenomenal, seductive power of television has done for them. Now that entertainment is beamed globally into people's heads without their having to speak to one another, the engine that generated the stories has finally run out of gas.

But perhaps not entirely. A recent television program told of the disasters that befell those men who, when erecting the first electrical power lines, were crass enough to plant them within the circle of a fairy fort. Likewise, there is no doubt that the "memory" of a past event can cling to a place and that a sensitive soul can resonate to that "memory," and become aware of it. So, I have tried to show that the landscape in the west still vibrates with the memory of the *Sidhe* and that, though they may never be seen again, if you know where, and how, to listen, you may just pick up a whisper of them.

In conclusion, though I have tried many times, I have never been able to photograph a fairy fort. Easy enough to record their images on film, but if you can't work at least a little of a place's poetry into an image, then that place has held on to its secrets. Fairy forts have refused to yield their secrets to me. One of these photographs, though, was taken from the raised rim of a fairy fort, looking outwards, and I like to think that in this—and in one or two of the others here—the *Sidhe* have allowed the fog that surrounds us now to thin a little bit, so we can infer a dim projection of how the world might look to them.

AT THE EDGE
OF THE WORLD

THE CROOKENED BACK

T. Crofton Croker

~

*P*eggy Barrett was once tall, well-shaped, and comely. She was in her youth remarkable for two qualities, not often found together, of being the most thrifty housewife, and the best dancer in her native village of Ballyhooley. But she is now upwards of sixty years old; and during the last ten years of her life, she has never been able to stand upright. Her back is bent nearly to a level; yet she has the freest use of all her limbs that can be enjoyed in such a posture; her health is good, and her mind vigorous; and, in the family of her eldest son, with whom she has lived since the death of her husband, she performs all the domestic services which her age, and the infirmity just mentioned, allow. She washes the potatoes, makes the fire, sweeps the house (labours in which she good-humouredly says, "she finds her crooked back mighty convenient"), plays with the children, and tells stories to the family and their neighbouring friends, who often collect round her son's fireside to hear them during the long winter evenings. Her powers of conversation are highly extolled, both for humour and narration; and anecdotes of droll or awkward incidents, connected with the posture in which she has been so long fixed, as well as the history of the occurrence to which she owes that misfortune, are the favourite topics of her discourse. Among other matters she is fond of relating how, on a certain day, at the close of a bad harvest, when several tenants of the estate on which she lived concerted in a field a petition for an abatement of rent, they placed the paper on which they wrote upon her back, which was found no very inconvenient substitute for a table.

Peggy, like all experienced storytellers, suited her tales, both in length and subject, to the audience and the occasion. She knew that, in broad daylight, when the sun shines brightly, and the trees are budding, and the birds singing around us, when men and women, like ourselves, are moving and speaking, employed variously in business or amusement—she knew, in short (though certainly without knowing or much caring wherefore), that when we are engaged about the realities of life and nature, we want that spirit of credulity, without which tales of the deepest interest will lose their power. At such times Peggy was brief, very particular as to facts, and never dealt in the marvellous. But round the blazing hearth of a Christmas evening, when infidelity is banished from all companies, at least in low and simple life, as a quality, to say the least of it, out of season; when the winds of "dark December" whistled bleakly round the walls, and almost through the doors of the little mansion, reminding its inmates that, as the world is vexed by elements superior to human power, so it may be visited by beings of a superior nature: at such times would Peggy Barrett give full scope to her memory, or her imagination, or both; and upon one of these occasions, she gave the following circumstantial account of the "crookening of her back."

"It was of all days in the year, the day before May-day, that I went out to the garden to weed the potatoes. I would not have gone out that day, but I was dull in myself, and sorrowful, and wanted to be alone; all the boys and girls were laughing and joking in the house, making goaling-balls and dressing out ribands for the mummers next day. I couldn't bear it. 'Twas only at the Easter that was then past (and that's ten years last Easter—I won't forget the time) that I buried my poor man; and I thought how gay and joyful I was, many a long year before that, at the May-eve before our wedding, when with Robin by my side, I sat cutting and sewing the ribands for the goaling-ball I was to give to the boys on the next day, proud to be preferred above all the other girls of the banks of the Blackwater by the handsomest boy and the best hurler in the village; so I left the house and went to the garden. I staid there all the day, and didn't come home to dinner. I don't know how it was, but somehow I continued on, weeding, and thinking sorrowfully enough, and singing over some of the old songs that I sung many and many a time in the days that are gone, and for them that never will come back to me to hear them. The truth is, I hated to go and sit silent and mournful among the people in the house that were merry and young, and had the best of their days before them. 'Twas late before I thought of returning home, and I did not leave the garden till some time after sunset. The moon was up; but though there wasn't a cloud to be seen, and though a star was winking here and there in the sky, the day wasn't long enough gone to have it clear moonlight; still it shone enough to make everything on one side of the heavens look pale and silvery-like; and the thin white mist was just beginning to creep along the fields. On the other side, near where the sun was set, there was more of daylight, and the sky looked angry, red and fiery through the trees, like as if it was lighted up by a great town burning below. Everything was as silent as a churchyard, only now and then one could hear far off a dog barking, or a cow lowing after being milked. There wasn't a creature to be seen on the road or in the fields, I wondered at this first, but then I remembered it was May-eve, and that many a thing, both good and bad, would be wandering about that night, and that I ought to shun danger as well as others. So I walked on as quick as I could, and soon came to the end of the demesne wall, where the trees rise high and thick at each side of the road, and almost meet at the top. My heart misgave me when I got under the shade. There was so much light let down from the opening above, that I could see about a stone throw before me. All of a sudden I heard a rustling among the branches, on the right side of the road, and saw something like a small black goat, only with long wide horns turned out instead of being bent backwards, standing upon its hind legs upon the top of the wall, and looking down on me. My breath stopped, and I couldn't move for near a minute. I couldn't help, somehow, keeping my eyes fixed on it; and it never stirred, but kept looking in the same fixed way down at me. At last I made a rush, and went on; but I didn't go ten steps, when I saw the very same sight, on the wall to the left of me, standing in exactly the same manner, but three or four times as high, and almost as tall as the tallest man. The horns looked frightful: it gazed upon me as before; my legs shook, and my teeth chattered, and I thought I would drop down dead every moment. At last I felt as if I was obliged to go on—and on I went; but it was without feeling how I moved or whether my legs carried me. Just as I passed the spot where this frightful thing was standing, I heard a noise as if something sprung from the wall, and felt as if a heavy animal plumped down upon me, and held with the fore feet clinging to my shoulder, and the hind ones fixed in my gown, that was folded and pinned up behind me. 'Tis the wonder of my life ever since how I bore the shock; but so it was, I neither fell, nor even staggered with the weight, but walked on as if I had the strength of ten men, though I felt as if I couldn't help moving, and couldn't stand still if I wished it. Though I gasped with fear, I knew as well as I do now what I was doing. I tried to cry out, but couldn't; I tried to run, but wasn't able; I tried to look back, but my head and neck were as if they were screwed in a vise. I could barely roll my eyes on each side, and then I could see, as clearly and plainly as if it was in the broad light of the blessed sun, a black and cloven foot planted upon each of my shoulders. I heard a low breathing in my ear; I felt, at every step I took, my leg strike back against the feet of the creature that was on my back. Still I could do nothing but walk straight on. At last I came within sight of the house, and a welcome sight it was to me, for I thought I would be released when I reached it. I soon came close to the door, but it was shut; I looked at the little window, but it was shut too, for they were more cautious about May-eve than I was; I saw the light inside, through the chinks of the door; I heard 'em talking and laughing within; I felt myself at three yards distance from them that would die to save me—and may the Lord save me from ever feeling what I did that night, when I found myself held by what couldn't be good nor friendly, but without the power to help myself, or to call my friends, or to put out my hand to knock, or even to lift my leg to strike the door, and let them know that I was outside it! 'Twas as if my hands grew to my sides, and my feet were glued to the ground, or had the weight of a rock fixed to them. At last I thought of blessing myself; and my right hand, that would do nothing else, did that for me. Still the weight remained on my back, and all was as before. I blessed myself again; 'twas still all the same. I then gave myself up for lost: but I blessed myself a third time, and my hand no sooner finished the sign, than all at once I felt the burthen spring off my back: the door flew open as if a clap of thunder burst it, and I was pitched forward on my forehead, in upon the middle of the floor. When I got up my back was crookened, and I never stood straight from that night to this blessed hour."

There was a pause when Peggy Barrett finished. Those who had heard the story before had listened with a look of half-satisfied interest, blenched, however, with an expression of that serious and solemn feeling, which always attends a tale of supernatural wonders, how often soever told. They moved upon their seats out of the posture in which they had remained fixed during the narrative, and sat in an attitude which denoted that their curiosity as to the cause of this strange occurrence had been long since allayed. Those to whom it was before unknown still retained their look and posture of strained attention, and anxious but solemn expectation. A grandson of Peggy's, about nine years old (not the child of the son with whom she lived), had never before heard the story. As it grew in interest, he was observed to cling closer and closer to the old woman's side; and at the close he was gazing steadfastly at her, with his body bent back across her knees, and his face turned up to hers, with a look, through which a disposition to weep seemed contending with curiosity. After a moment's pause, he could no longer restrain his impatience, and catching her grey locks in one hand, while the tear of dread and wonder was just dropping from his eye-lash, he cried, "Granny, what was it?"

The old woman smiled first at the elder part of her audience, and then at her grandson, and patting him on the forehead, she said, "It was the Phooka."

7

FERGUS O'MARA
AND THE AIR-DEMONS

P. W. Joyce

~

Of all the different kinds of goblins that haunted the lonely places of Ireland in days of old, air-demons were most dreaded by the people. They lived among the clouds, and mists, and rocks, and they hated the human race with the utmost malignity. In those times lived in the north of Desmond (the present country of Cork) a man named Fergus O'Mara. His farm lay on the southern slope of the Ballyhoura Mountains, along which ran the open road that led to his house. This road was not shut in by walls or fences; but on both sides there were scattered trees and bushes that sheltered it in winter, and made it dark and gloomy when you approached the house at night. Beside the road, a little way off from the house, there was a spot that had an evil name all over the country, a little hill covered closely with copsewood with a great craggy rock on top, from which, on stormy nights, strange and fearful sounds had often been heard—shrill voices, and screams, mingled with loud fiendish laughter; and the people believed that it was the haunt of air-demons. In some way it had become known that these demons had an eye on Fergus, and watched for every opportunity to get him into their power. He had himself been warned of this many years before, by an old monk from the neighbouring monastery of Buttevant, who told him, moreover, that so long as he led a blameless, upright life, he need have no fear of the demons; but if ever he yielded to temptation or fell into any great sin, then would come the opportunity for which they were watching day and night. He never forgot this warning, and he was very careful to keep himself straight, both because he was naturally a good man, and for fear of the air-demons.

Some time before the occurrence about to be related, one of Fergus's children, a sweet little girl about seven years of age, fell ill and died. The little thing gradually wasted away, but suffered no pain; and as she became weaker she became more loving and gentle than ever, and talked in a wonderful way, quite beyond her years, of the bright land she was going to. One thing she was particularly anxious about, that when she was dying they should let her hold a blessed candle in her hand. They thought it was very strange that she should be continually thinking and talking of this; and over and over again she made her father and mother promise that it should be done. And with the blessed candle in her hand she died so calmly and sweetly that those around her could not tell the exact moment.

About a year after this, on a bright Sunday morning in October, Fergus set out for Mass. The place was about three miles away, and it was not a chapel, but a lonely old fort, called to this day Lissanaffrin, the fort of the Mass. A rude stone altar stood at one side of the mound of the fort, under a little shed that sheltered the priest also; and the congregation worshipped in the open air on the green plot in the centre. For in those days there were many places that had no chapels; and the people flocked to see these open-air Masses as faithfully as we do now to our stately, comfortable chapels. The family had gone on before, the men walking and the women and children riding; and Fergus set out to walk alone.

Just as he approached the Demons' Rock he was greatly surprised to hear the eager yelping of dogs, and in a moment a great deer bounded from a covert beside the rock, with three hounds after her in full chase. No man in the whole country round loved a good chase better than Fergus, or had a swifter foot to follow, and without a moment's hesitation he started in pursuit.

But in a few minutes he stopped up short; for he bethought him of the Mass, and there was little time for delay. While he stood wavering, the deer seemed to slacken her pace, and the hounds gained on her, and in a moment Fergus dashed off at full speed, forgetting Mass and everything else in his eagerness for the sport. But it turned out a long and weary chase. Sometimes they slackened, and he was almost at the hounds' tails, but the next moment both deer and hounds darted forward and he was left far behind. Sometimes they were in full view, and again they were out of sight in thickets and deep glens, so that he could guide himself only by the cry of the hounds. In this way he was decoyed across hills and glens, but instead of gaining ground he found himself rather falling behind.

Mass was all over and the people dispersed to their homes, and all wondered that they did not see Fergus; for no one could remember that he was ever absent before. His wife returned expecting to find him at home; but when she arrived there was trouble in her heart, for there were no tidings of him, and no one had seen him since he had set out for Mass in the morning.

Meantime Fergus followed up the chase till he was wearied out; and at last, just on the edge of a wild moor, both deer and hounds disappeared behind a shoulder of rock, and he lost them altogether. At the same moment the cry of the hounds became changed to frightful shrieks and laughter, such as he had heard more than once from Demons' Rock. And now, sitting down to rest, he had full time to reflect on what he had done, and was overwhelmed with remorse and shame. Moreover, his heart sank within him, thinking of the last sound he had heard; for he believed that he had been allured from Mass by the cunning wiles of the demons and he feared his home, hoping to reach it before night. But before he had got half-way, night fell and a storm came on, great wind and rain, and bursts of thunder and lightning. Fergus was strong and active, however, and knew every turn of the mountain, and he made his way through the storm until he approached the Demons' Rock.

Suddenly there burst on his ears the very same sounds that he had heard on losing sight of the chase—shouts and shrieks of laughter. A great black ragged cloud, whirling round and round with furious gusts of wind, burst from

the rock and came sweeping and tearing towards him. Crossing himself in terror and uttering a short prayer, he rushed for home. But the whirlwind swept
nearer, till at last, in a sort of dim, shadowy light, he saw the black cloud full of
frightful faces, all glaring straight at him and coming closer and closer. At this
moment a bright light dropped down from the sky and rested in front of the

cloud; and when he looked up, he saw his little child floating in the air before him and the demons, holding a lighted candle in her hand. And though the storm was raging and roaring all round, she was quite calm—not a breath of air stirred her long yellow hair and the candle burned quietly. Even in the midst of all his terror he could observe her pale, gentle face and blue eyes just as when she was alive, not showing traces of sickness or sadness now, but lighted up with joy. The demons seemed to start back from the light, and with great uproar, rushed round to the other side of Fergus, the black cloud still moving with them and wrapping them up in its ragged folds; but the little angel still floated softly round, keeping between them and her father. Fergus ran on for home, and the cloud of demons still kept furiously whirling round and round him, bringing with them the roots; but still the child, always holding the candle towards them, kept floating calmly round and shielded him.

At length he arrived at his house; the door lay half open, for the family were inside expecting him home, listening with wonder and affright to the approaching noises; and he bounded in through the doorway and fell flat on his face. That instant the door—though no one was near—was shut violently, and the bolts were shot home. They hurried anxiously round him, to lift him up, but found him in a death-like swoon. Meantime the uproar outside became greater than ever; round and round the house it tore, a roaring whirlwind with shouts and yells of rage, and great trampling, as if there was a whole company of horsemen. At length, however, the noises seemed to move away farther and farther off from the house, and gradually died away in the distance. At the same time the storm ceased, and the night became calm and beautiful.

The daylight was shining in through the windows when Fergus recovered from his swoon, and then he told his fearful story; but many days passed over before he had quite recovered from the horrors of that night. When the family came forth in the morning there was fearful waste all round and near the house, trees and bushes torn from the roots, and the ground all trampled and torn up. After this the revelry of the demons was never again heard from the rock; and it was believed that they had left it and betaken themselves to some other haunt.

THE EVIL EYE

Lady Wilde

~

*T*here is nothing more dreaded by the people, nor considered more deadly in its effects, than the Evil Eye.

It may strike at any moment unless the greatest precautions are taken, and even then there is no true help possible unless the fairy doctor is at once summoned to pronounce the mystic charm that can alone destroy the evil and fatal influence.

There are several modes in which the Evil Eye can act, some much more deadly than others. If certain persons are met the first thing in the morning, you will be unlucky for the whole of that day in all you do. If the evil-eyed comes in to rest, and looks fixedly on anything, on cattle or on a child, there is doom in the glance, a fatality which cannot be evaded except by a powerful counter-charm. But if the evil-eyed mutters a verse over a sleeping child, that child will assuredly die, for the incantation is of the devil, and no charm has power to resist it or turn away the evil. Sometimes the process of bewitching is effected by looking fixedly at the object, through nine fingers; especially is the magic fatal if the victim is seated by the fire in the evening when the moon is full. Therefore, to avoid being suspected of having the Evil Eye, it is necessary at once, when looking at a child, to say "God bless it." And when passing a farmyard where the cows are collected for milking, to say, "The blessing of God be on you and on all your labours." If this form is omitted, the worst results may be apprehended, and the people would be filled with terror and alarm, unless a counter-charm were not instantly employed.

The singular malific influence of a glance has been felt by most persons in life; an influence that seems to paralyze intellect and speech, simply by the mere presence in the room of someone who is mystically antipathetic to our nature. For the soul is like a fine-toned harp that vibrates to the slightest external force or movement, and the presence and glance of some persons can radiate around us in a divine joy, while others may kill the soul with a sneer or a frown. We call these subtle influences mysteries, but the early races believed them to be produced by spirits, good or evil, as they acted on the nerves or on the intellect.

Some years ago an old woman was living in Kerry, and it was thought so unlucky to meet her in the morning that all the girls used to go out after sunset to bring in water for the following day, that so they might avoid her evil glance; for whatever she looked on came to loss and grief.

There was a man, also, equally dreaded on account of the strange, fatal power of his glance; and so many accidents and misfortunes were traced to his presence that finally the neighbours insisted that he should wear a black patch over the Evil Eye, not to be removed unless by request; for learned gentlemen, curious in such things, sometimes came to him to ask for a proof of his power, and he would try it for a wager while drinking with his friends.

One day, near an old ruin of a castle, he met a boy weeping in great grief for his pet pigeon, which had got up to the very top of the ruin, and could not be coaxed down.

"What will you give me," asked the man, "if I bring it down for you?"

"I have nothing to give," said the boy, "but I will pray to God for you. Only get me back my pigeon, and I shall be happy."

Then the man took off the black patch and looked up steadfastly at the bird; when all of a sudden it fell to the ground and lay motionless, as if stunned; but there was no harm done to it, and the boy took it up and went his way rejoicing.

A woman in the County Galway had a beautiful child, so handsome, that all the neighbours were very careful to say "God bless it" when they saw him, for they knew the fairies would desire to steal the child, and carry it off to the hills.

But one day it chanced that an old woman, a stranger, came in. "Let me rest," she said, "for I am weary." And she sat down and looked at the child, but never said "God bless it." And when she had rested, she rose up, looked again at the child fixedly, in silence, and then went her way.

All that night the child cried and would not sleep. And all next day it moaned as if in pain. So the mother told the priest, but he would do nothing for fear of the fairies. And just as the poor mother was in despair, she saw a strange woman going by the door. "Who knows," she said to her husband, "but this woman would help us." So they asked her to come in and rest. And when she looked at the child she said, "God bless it," instantly, and spat three times at it, and then sat down.

"Now what will you give me," she said, "if I tell you what ails the child?"

"I will cross your hand with silver," said the mother, "as much as you want, only speak," and she laid the money on the woman's hand. "Now tell me the truth, for the sake and in the name of Mary and the good angels."

"Well," said the stranger, "the fairies have had your child these two days in the hills, and this is a changeling they have left in its place. But so many blessings were said on your child that the fairies can do it no harm. For there was only one blessing wanting, and only one person gave the Evil Eye. Now, you must watch for this woman, carry her into the house and secretly cut off a piece of her cloak. Then burn the piece close to the child, till the smoke as it rises makes him sneeze; and when this happens the spell is broken, and your own child will come back to you safe and sound, in place of the changeling."

Then the stranger rose up and went on her way.

All that evening the mother watched for the old woman, and at last she spied her on the road. "Come in," she cried, "come in, good woman, and rest, for the cakes are hot on the griddle, and supper is ready."

So the woman came in, but never said "God bless you kindly" to man or mortal, only scowled at the child, who cried worse than ever.

Now the mother had told her eldest girl to cut off a piece of the old woman's cloak, secretly, when she sat down to eat. And the girl did as she was desired, and handed the piece to her mother, unknown to any one. But, to their surprise, this was no sooner done than the woman rose up and went out without uttering a word; and they saw her no more.

Then the father carried the child outside, and burned the piece of cloth before the door, and held the boy over the smoke till he sneezed three times violently; after which he gave the child back to the mother, who laid him in his bed, where he slept peacefully, with a smile on his face, and cried no more with the cry of pain. And when he woke up, the mother knew that she had got her own darling child back from the fairies, and no evil thing happened to him any more.

It was believed that the power of fascination by the glance, which is not necessarily an evil power like the Evil Eye, was possessed in a remarkable degree by learned and wise people, especially poets, so that they could make themselves loved and followed by any girl they liked, simply by the influence of the glance. About the year 1790, a young man resided in the County Limerick, who had this power in a singular and unusual degree. He was a clever, witty rhymer in the Irish language; and probably had the deep poet eyes that characterize warm and passionate poet natures, eyes that even without necromancy have been known to exercise a powerful magnetic influence over female minds.

One day, while travelling far from home, he came upon a bright, pleasant-looking farmhouse, and feeling weary, he stopped and requested a drink of milk and leave to rest. The farmer's daughter, a young, handsome girl, not liking to admit a stranger, as all the maids were churning, and she was alone in the house, refused him admittance.

The young poet fixed his eyes earnestly on her face for some time in silence, then slowly turning round left the house, and walked towards a small grove of trees just opposite. There he stood for a few moments resting against a tree, and facing the house as if to take one last vengeful or admiring glance, then went on his way without turning round.

The young girl had been watching him from the windows, and the moment he moved she passed out of the door like one in a dream, and followed him slowly, step by step, down the avenue. The maids grew alarmed, and called to her father, who ran out and shouted loudly for her to stop, but she never turned or seemed to heed. The young man, however, looked round, and seeing the whole family in pursuit, quickened his pace, first glancing fixedly at the girl for a moment.

Immediately she sprang towards him, and they were both almost out of sight, when one of the maids espied a piece of paper tied to a branch of the tree where the poet had rested. From curiosity she took it down, and the moment the knot was untied, the farmer's daughter suddenly stopped, became quite still, and when her father came up she allowed him to lead her back to the house without resistance.

When questioned, she said that she felt herself drawn by an invisible force to follow the young stranger wherever he might lead, and that she would have followed him through the world, for her life seemed bound up in his; she had no will to resist, and was conscious of nothing else but his presence. Suddenly, however, the spell was broken, and then she heard her father's voice and knew how strangely she had acted. At the same time the power of the young man over her vanished, and the impulse to follow him was no longer in her heart.

The paper, on being opened, was found to contain five mysterious words written in blood, and in this order—

Sator
Arepo
Tenet
Opera
Rotas

These letters are so arranged that read in any way, right to left, left to right, up or down, the same words are produced; and when written in blood with a pen made of an eagle's feather, they form a charm which no woman (it is said) can resist; but the incredulous reader can easily test the truth of this assertion for himself.

THE STUDENT WHO LEFT COLLEGE

Douglas Hyde

~

*T*here came a number of young people from the County of Galway to a great college, to learn and gain instruction, so as to become priests. I often heard the name of this college from my mother, but I do not remember it. It was not Maynooth. There was a man of these of the name of Patrick O'Flynn. He was the son of a rich farmer. His father and his mother desired to make a priest of him. He was a nice, gentle lad. He used not to go dancing with the other boys in the evening, but it was his habit to go out with the grey-light of day, and he used to be walking by himself up and down under the shadow of the great trees that were round about the college, and he used to remain there thinking and meditating by himself, until some person would come and bring him into his room.

One evening, in the month of May, he went out, as was his custom, and he was taking his walk under the trees when he heard a melodious music. There came a darkness or a sort of blindness over his eyes, and when he found his sight again he beheld a great high wall on every side of him, and out in front of him a shining road. The musicians were on the road, and they playing melodiously, and he heard a voice saying, "Come with us to the land of delight and rest." He looked back and beheld a great high wall behind him and on each side of him, and he was not able to return back again across the wall, although he desired to return. He went forward then after the music. He did not know how long he walked, but the great high wall kept ever on each side of him and behind him.

He was going, and ever-going, until they came to a great river, and water in it as red as blood. Wonder came upon him then, and great fear. But the musicians walked across the river without wetting their feet, and Patrick O'Flynn followed them without wetting his own. He thought at first that the musicians belonged to the Fairy-Host, and next he thought that he had died and that it was a group of angels that were in it, taking him to heaven.

The walls fell away from them then, on each side, and they came to a great wide plain. They were going then, and ever-going, until they came to a fine castle that was in the midst of the plain. The musicians went in, but Patrick O'Flynn remained outside. It was not long until the chief of the musicians came out to him and brought him into a handsome chamber. He spoke not a word, and Patrick O'Flynn never heard one word spoken so long as he remained there.

There was no night in that place, but the light of day throughout. He never ate and he never drank a single thing there, and he never saw anyone eating or drinking, and the music never ceased. Every half-hour, as he thought, he used to hear a bell, as it were a church-bell being rung, but he never beheld the bell, and he was unable to see it in any place.

When the musicians used to go out upon the plain before the castle, there used to come a tribe of every sort of bird in the heavens, playing the most melodious music that ear ever heard. It was often Patrick O'Flynn said to himself, "It is certain that I am in heaven, but is it not curious that I have no remembrance of sickness, nor of death, nor of judgement, and that I have not seen God nor his Blessed Mother, as is promised to us?"

Patrick O'Flynn did not know how long he was in that delightful place. He thought that he had been in it only for a short little time, but he was in it for a hundred years and one.

One day the musicians were out in the field and he was listening to them, when the chief came to him. He brought him out and put him behind the musicians. They departed on their way, and they made neither stop nor stay until they came to the river that was as red as blood. They went across that, without wetting their foot-soles, and went forward until they came to the field near the college where they found him at the first. Then they departed out of his sight like a mist.

He looked round him, and recognized the college, but he thought that the trees were higher and that there was some change in the college itself. He went in, then, but he did not recognise a single person whom he met, and not a person recognized him.

The principal of the college came to him, and said to him, "Where are you from, son, or what is your name?"

"I am Patrick O'Flynn from the County of Galway," said he.

"How long are you here?" said the principal.

"I am here since the first day of March," said he.

"I think that you are out of your senses," said the principal, "there is no person of your name in the college, and there has not been for twenty years, for I am more than twenty years here."

"Though you were in it since you were born, yet I am here since last March, and I can show you my room and my books."

With that he went up the stairs, and the principal after him. He went into his room and looked round him, and said, "This is my room, but that is not my furniture, and those are not my books that are in it." He saw an old Bible upon the table and he opened it, and said: "This is my Bible—my mother gave it to me when I was coming here; and, see, my name is written in it."

The principal looked at the Bible, and there, as sure as God is in heaven, was the name of Patrick O'Flynn written in it, and the day of the month that he left home.

Now there was great trouble of mind on the principal, and he did not know what he should do. He sent for the masters and the professors and he told them the story.

"By my word," said an old priest that was in it, "I heard talk when I was young, of a student who went away out of this college, and there was no account of him since, whether living or dead. The people searched the river and the bog holes, but there was no account to be had of him, and they never got the body."

The principal called to them then and bade them bring him a great book in which the name of every person was written who had come to that college since it was founded. He looked through the book, and see! Patrick O'Flynn's name was in it, and the day of the month that he came, and this (note) was written opposite to his name, that the same Patrick O'Flynn had departed on such a day, and that nobody knew what had become of him. Now it was exactly one hundred and one years from the day he went until the day he came back in that fashion.

"This is a wonderful, and a very wonderful story," said the principal, "but, do you wait here quietly, my son," said he, "and I shall write to the bishop." He did that, and he got an account from the bishop to keep the man until he should come himself.

At the end of a week after that the bishop came and sent for Patrick O'Flynn. There was nobody present except the two. "Now, son," said the bishop, "go on your knees and make a confession." Then he made an act of contrition, and the bishop gave him absolution.

Immediately there came a fainting and a heavy sleep over him, and he was, as it were, for three days and three nights a dead person. When he came to himself the bishop and priests were round about him. He rose up, shook himself, and told them his story, as I have told it, and he put excessive wonder upon every man of them. "Now," said he, "here I am alive and safe, and do as ye please."

The bishop and the priests took counsel together. "It is a saintly man you are," said the bishop then, "and we shall give you holy orders on the spot."

They made a priest of him then, and no sooner were holy orders given him than he fell dead upon the altar, and they all heard at the same time the most melodious music that ear ever listened to, above them in the sky, and they all said that it was the angels who were in it, carrying the soul of Father O'Flynn up to heaven with them.

THE MAGIC SHIP

Séan O'Dubhda

❧

*F*ishing for mackerel we were in autumn; it is now more than forty years ago. It was a very fine night with no clouds to obscure the stars; it was in no wise dark. There were three of us—two of ourselves and another Murphy from the village, a son of the man called Uibh Rathac, he was a youth. It was past midnight, one or two o'clock perhaps, and we had set the mouth of Cuas na Ceannaine, east of the Ceanna itself. The six nets were stretched westwards and out to sea and we were at the inner end. The three of us saw her together—a large ship in full sail. She lay between us and Mionan about fifty spades away (about a hundred paces)—like a jet-black tower (of cloud). She was not far from the cliff as the point of the Mionan ran farther out than we were. We were afraid, naturally, and said to each other that we had better haul the nets and run. Another man said to leave them, for we would be moving towards the ship in the hauling, which we did not wish to do. She was nearer the tail nets than the inboard ones. We did not know what to do and young Murphy was very much afraid. Another canoe had cast north of us, between us and Binn Point, and he was screaming and shouting at them:

"You, over there, come and help us," for he thought that the ship would pounce on us suddenly. The three of us were frightened enough. The ship was not moving, she was so high above us that you would have to look upwards to see the tops of her sails. There she was without a move, standing like a jet-black mass up out of the water right to the top. She showed no light, neither did we see anybody on board nor hear a sound or a word. She appeared very strange to us but our fear was abating when she did not approach us. We left the nets set; there was no heavy sea or current—there never is during neap tides. She remained there for a good half hour. She remained there as long as that before she began to melt away. Then she began to grow smaller, the top part disappearing first. She began growing smaller and smaller and smaller till she appeared to be no bigger than a boat. She was no bigger than a canoe just before she melted (vanished) altogether. We stayed till morning but I think we had no good catch. We met a couple of other canoes that had been fishing about the same place and they had not seen her at all.

THE SOUL CAGES

T. Crofton Croker

~

*J*ack Dogherty lived on the coast of the county Clare. Jack was a fisherman, as his father and grandfather before him had been. Like them, too, he
lived all alone (but for the wife), and just in the same spot. People used to wonder why the Dogherty family were so fond of that wild situation, so far away
from all human kind, and in the midst of huge shattered rocks, with nothing
but the wide ocean to look upon. But they had their own good reasons for it.

The place was just the only spot on that part of the coast where anybody
could well live. There was a neat little creek, where a boat might lie as snug as
a puffin in her nest, and out from this creek a ledge of sunken rocks ran into
the sea. Now when the Atlantic, according to custom, was raging with a storm,
and a good westerly wind was blowing strong on the coast, many a richly-laden
ship went to pieces on these rocks; and then the fine bales of cotton and
tobacco, and such like things, and the pipes of wine and the puncheons of
rum, and the casks of brandy, and the kegs of Hollands that used to come
ashore! Dunbeg Bay was just like a little estate to the Doghertys.

Not but they were kind and humane to a distressed sailor, if ever one had the good luck to get to land; and many a time indeed did Jack put out in his little *corragh* (which, though not quite equal to honest Andrew Hennessy's canvas life-boat would breast the billows like any gannet), to lend a hand towards bringing off the crew from a wreck. But when the ship had gone to pieces, and the crew were all lost, who would blame Jack for picking up all he could find?

"And who is the worse of it?" said he. "For as to the king, God bless him! everybody knows he's rich enough already without getting what's floating in the sea."

Jack, though such a hermit, was a good-natured, jolly fellow. No other, sure, could ever have coaxed Biddy Mahony to quit her father's snug and warm house in the middle of the town of Ennis, and to go so many miles off to live among the rocks, with the seals and sea-gulls for next-door neighbours. But Biddy knew that Jack was the man for a woman who wished to be comfortable and happy; for to say nothing of the fish, Jack had the supplying of half the gentlemen's houses of the country with the *Godsends* that came into the bay. And she was right in her choice; for no woman ate, drank, or slept better, or made a prouder appearance at chapel on Sundays, than Mrs. Dogherty.

Many a strange sight, it may well be supposed, did Jack see, and many a strange sound did he hear, but nothing daunted him. So far was he from being afraid of Merrows, or such beings, that the very first wish of his heart was to fairly meet with one. Jack had heard that they were mighty like Christians, and that luck had always come out of an acquaintance with them. Never, therefore, did he dimly discern the Merrows moving along the face of the waters in their robes of mist, but he made direct for them; and many a scolding did Biddy, in her own quiet way, bestow upon Jack for spending his whole day out at sea, and bringing home no fish. Little did poor Biddy know the fish Jack was after!

It was rather annoying to Jack that, though living in a place where the Merrows were as plenty as lobsters, he never could get a right view of one. What vexed him more was that both his father and grandfather had often and often seen them; and he even remembered hearing, when a child, how his grandfather, who was the first of the family that had settled down at the creek, had been so intimate with a Merrow that, only for fear of vexing the priest, he would have had him stand for one of his children. This, however, Jack did not well know how to believe.

Fortune at length began to think that it was only right that Jack should know as much as his father and grandfather did. Accordingly, one day when he had strolled a little farther than usual along the coast to the northward, just as he turned a point, he saw something, like to nothing he had ever seen before, perched upon a rock at a little distance out to sea. It looked green in the body, as well as he could discern at that distance, and he would have sworn, only the thing was impossible, that it had a cocked hat in its hand. Jack stood for a good half hour straining his eyes, and wondering at it, and all the time the thing did not stir hand or foot. At last Jack's patience was quite worn out, and he gave a loud whistle and a hail, when the Merrow (for such it was) started up, put the cocked hat on its head, and dived down, head foremost, from the rock.

Jack's curiosity was now excited, and he constantly directed his steps towards the point; still he could never get a glimpse of the sea-gentleman with the cocked hat; and with thinking and thinking about the matter, he began at last to fancy he had been only dreaming. One very rough day, however, when the sea was running mountains high, Jack Dogherty determined to give a look at the Merrow's rock (for he had always chosen a fine day before), and then he saw the strange thing cutting capers upon the top of the rock, and then diving down, and then coming up, and then diving down again.

Jack had now only to choose his time (that is, a good blowing day), and he might see the man of the sea as often as he pleased. All this, however, did not satisfy him—"much will have more"; he wished now to get acquainted with the Merrow, and even in this he succeeded. One tremendous blustering day, before he got to the point whence he had a view of the Merrow's rock, the storm came on so furiously that Jack was obliged to take shelter in one of the caves which are so numerous along the coast; and there, to his astonishment, he saw sitting before him a thing with green hair, long green teeth, a red nose, and pig's eyes. It had a fish's tail, legs with scales on them, and short arms like fins. It wore no clothes, but had the cocked hat under its arm, and seemed engaged thinking very seriously about something.

Jack, with all his courage, was a little daunted; but now or never, thought he; so up he went boldly to the cogitating fishman, took off his hat, and made his best bow.

"Your servant, sir," said Jack.

"Your servant, kindly, Jack Dogherty," answered the Merrow.

"To be sure, then, how well your honour knows my name!" said Jack.

"Is it I not know your name, Jack Dogherty? Why, man, I knew your grandfather long before he was married to Judy Regan, your grandmother! Ah, Jack, Jack, I was fond of that grandfather of yours; he was a mighty worthy man in his time: I never met his match above or below, before or since, for sucking in a shellful of brandy. I hope, my boy," said the old fellow, with a merry twinkle in his eyes, "I hope you're his own grandson!"

"Never fear me for that," said Jack; "if my mother had only reared me on brandy, 'tis myself that would be a sucking infant to this hour!"

"Well, I like to hear you talk so manly; you and I must be better acquainted, if it were only for your grandfather's sake. But, Jack, that father of yours was not the thing! he had no head at all."

"I'm sure," said Jack, "since your honour lives down under the water, you must be obliged to drink a power to keep any heat in you in such a cruel, damp, *could* place. Well, I've often heard of Christians drinking like fishes; and might I be so bold as ask where you get the spirits?"

"Where do you get them yourself, Jack?" said the Merrow, twitching his red nose between his forefinger and thumb.

"Hubbubboo," cries Jack, "now I see how it is; but I suppose, sir, your honour has got a fine dry cellar below to keep them in."

"Let me alone for the cellar," said the Merrow, with a knowing wink of his left eye.

"I'm sure," continued Jack, "it must be mighty well worth the looking at."

"You may say that, Jack," said the Merrow; "and if you meet me here next Monday, just at this time of the day, we will have a little more talk with one another about the matter."

Jack and the Merrow parted the best friends in the world. On Monday they met, and Jack was not a little surprised to see that the Merrow had two cocked hats with him, one under each arm.

"Might I take the liberty to ask, sir," said Jack, "why your honour has brought the two hats with you to-day? You would not, sure, be going to give me one of them, to keep for the *curiosity* of the thing?"

"No, no, Jack," said he, "I don't get my hats so easily, to part with them that way; but I want you to come down and dine with me, and I brought you that hat to dine with."

"Lord bless and preserve us!" cried Jack, in amazement, "would you want me to go down to the bottom of the salt sea ocean? Sure, I'd be smothered and choked up with the water, to say nothing of being drowned! And what would poor Biddy do for me, and what would she say?"

"And what matter what she says, you *pinkeen?* Who cares for Biddy's squalling? It's long before your grandfather would have talked in that way. Many's the time he stuck that same hat on his head, and dived down boldly after me; and many's the snug bit of dinner and good shellful of brandy he and I have had together below, under the water."

"Is it really, sir, and no joke?" said Jack; "why, then, sorrow from me for ever and a day after, if I'll be a bit worse man nor my grandfather was! Here goes—but play me fair now. Here's neck or nothing!" cried Jack.

"That's your grandfather all over," said the old fellow; "so come along, then, and do as I do."

They both left the cave, walked into the sea, and then swam a piece until they got to the rock. The Merrow climbed to the top of it, and Jack followed him. On the far side it was as straight as the wall of a house, and the sea beneath looked so deep that Jack was almost cowed.

"Now, do you see, Jack," said the Merrow: "just put this hat on your head, and mind to keep your eyes wide open. Take hold of my tail, and follow me, and you'll see what you'll see."

In he dashed, and in dashed Jack after him boldly. They went and they went, and Jack thought they'd never stop going. Many a time did he wish himself sitting at home by the fireside with Biddy. Yet where was the use of wishing now, when he was so many miles, as he thought, below the waves of the Atlantic? Still he held hard by the Merrow's tail, slippery as it was; and, at last, to Jack's great surprise, they got out of the water, and he actually found himself on dry land at the bottom of the sea. They landed just in front of a nice house that was slated very neatly with oyster shells! And the Merrow, turning about to Jack, welcomed him down.

Jack could hardly speak, what with wonder, and what with being out of breath with travelling so fast through the water. He looked about him and could see no living things, barring crabs and lobsters, of which there were plenty walking leisurely about on the sand. Overhead was the sea like a sky, and the fishes like birds swimming about in it.

"Why don't you speak, man?" said the Merrow: "I dare say you had no notion that I had such a snug little concern here as this? Are you smothered, or choked, or drowned, or are you fretting after Biddy, eh?"

"Oh! not myself indeed," said Jack, showing his teeth with a good-humoured grin; "but who in the world would ever have thought of seeing such a thing?"

"Well, come along, and let's see what they've got for us to eat?"

Jack really was hungry, and it gave him no small pleasure to perceive a fine column of smoke rising from the chimney, announcing what was going on within. Into the house he followed the Merrow, and there he saw a good kitchen, right well provided with everything. There was a noble dresser, and plenty of pots and pans, with two young Merrows cooking. His host then led him into the room, which was furnished shabbily enough. Not a table or a chair was there in it; nothing but planks and logs of wood to sit on, and eat off. There was, however, a good fire blazing upon the hearth—a comfortable sight to Jack.

"Come now, and I'll show you where I keep—you know what," said the

Merrow, with a sly look; and opening a little door, he led Jack into a fine cellar, well filled with pipes, and kegs, and hogsheads, and barrels.

"What do you say to that, Jack Dogherty? Eh! may be a body can't live snug under the water?"

"Never the doubt of that," said Jack, with a convincing smack of his upper lip, that he really thought what he said.

They went back to the room, and found dinner laid. There was no table-cloth, to be sure—but what matter? It was not always Jack had one at home. The dinner would have been no discredit to the first house of the country on a fast day. The choicest of fish, and no wonder, was there. Turbots, and sturgeons, and soles, and lobsters, and oysters, and twenty other kinds, were on the planks at once, and plenty of the best of foreign spirits. The wines, the old fellow said, were too cold for his stomach.

Jack ate and drank till he could eat no more; then, taking up a shell of brandy, "Here's to your honour's good health, sir," said he; "though, begging your pardon, it's mighty odd that as long as we've been acquainted I don't know your name yet."

"That's true, Jack," replied he; "I never thought of it before, but better late than never. My name's Coomara."

"And a mighty decent name it is," cried Jack, taking another shellful: "here's to your health, Coomara, and may ye live these fifty years to come!"

"Fifty years!" repeated Coomara; "I'm obliged to you, indeed! If you had said five hundred, it would have been something worth the wishing."

"By the laws, sir," cries Jack, "*youz* live to a powerful age here under the water! You knew my grandfather, and he's dead and gone better than these sixty years. I'm sure it must be a healthy place to live in."

"No doubt of it; but come, Jack, keep the liquor stirring."

Shell after shell did they empty, and to Jack's exceeding surprise, he found the drink never got into his head, owing, I suppose, to the sea being over them, which kept their noodles cool.

Old Coomara got exceedingly comfortable, and sung several songs; but Jack, if his life had depended on it, never could remember more than

Rum fum boodle boo,

Ripple dipple nitty dob;

Dumdoo doodle coo,

Raffle taffle chittiboo!

It was the chorus to one of them; and, to say the truth, nobody that I know has ever been able to pick any particular meaning out of it; but that, to be sure, is the case with many a song nowadays.

At length said he to Jack, "Now, my dear boy, if you follow me, I'll show you my *curiosities!*" He opened a little door, and led Jack into a large room, where Jack saw a great many odds and ends that Coomara had picked up at one time or another. What chiefly took his attention, however, were things like lobster-pots ranged on the ground along the wall.

"Well, Jack, how do you like my *curiosities?*" said old Coo.

"Upon my *sowkins,* sir," said Jack, "they're mighty well worth the looking at; but might I make so bold as to ask what these things like lobster-pots are?"

"Oh! the Soul Cages, is it?"

"The what? sir!"

"These things here that I keep the souls in."

"*Arrah!* what souls, sir?" said Jack, in amazement; "sure the fish have no souls in them?"

"Oh! no," replied Coo, quite coolly, "that they have not; but these are the souls of drowned sailors."

"The Lord preserve us from all harm!" muttered Jack, "how in the world did you get them?"

"Easily enough: I've only, when I see a good storm coming on, to set a couple of dozen of these, and then, when the sailors are drowned and the souls get out of them under the water, the poor things are almost perished to death, not being used to the cold; so they make into my pots for shelter, and then I have them snug, and fetch them home, and keep them here dry and warm; and is it not well for them, poor souls, to get into such good quarters?"

Jack was so thunderstruck he did not know what to say, so he said nothing. They went back into the dining-room, and had a little more brandy, which was excellent, and then, as Jack knew that it must be getting late, and as Biddy might be uneasy, he stood up, and said he thought it was time for him to be on the road.

"Just as you like, Jack," said Coo, "but take a *duc an durrus* before you go; you've a cold journey before you."

Jack knew better manners than to refuse the parting glass. "I wonder," said he, "will I be able to make out my way home?"

"What should ail you," said Coo, "when I'll show you the way?"

Out they went before the house, and Coomara took one of the cocked hats, and put it upon Jack's head the wrong way, and then lifted him up on his shoulder that he might launch him up into the water.

"Now," says he, giving him a heave, "you'll come up just in the same spot you came down in; and, Jack, mind and throw me back the hat."

He canted Jack off his shoulder, and up he shot like a bubble—whirr, whirr, whiz—away he went up through the water, till he came to the very rock he had jumped off, where he found a landing-place, and then in he threw the hat, which sunk like a stone.

The sun was just going down in the beautiful sky of a calm summer's evening. *Feascor* was seen dimly twinkling in the cloudless heaven, a solitary star, and the waves of the Atlantic flashed in a golden flood of light. So Jack, perceiving it was late, set off home; but when he got there, not a word did he say to Biddy of where he had spent his day.

The state of the poor souls cooped up in the lobster-pots gave Jack a great deal of trouble, and how to release them cost him a great deal of thought. He at first had a mind to speak to the priest about the matter. But what could the priest do, and what did Coo care for the priest? Besides, Coo was a good sort of an old fellow, and did not think he was doing any harm. Jack had a regard for him, too, and it also might not be much to his own credit if it were known that he used to go dine with Merrows. On the whole, he thought his best plan would be to ask Coo to dinner, and to make him drunk, if he was able, and then to take the hat and go down and turn up the pots. It was, first of all, necessary, however, to get Biddy out of the way; for Jack was prudent enough, as she was a woman, to wish to keep the thing secret from her.

Accordingly, Jack grew mighty pious all of a sudden, and said to Biddy that he thought it would be for the good of both their souls if she was to go and take her rounds at Saint John's Well, near Ennis. Biddy thought so too, and accordingly off she set one fine morning at day-dawn, giving Jack a strict charge to have an eye to the place. The coast being clear, away went Jack to the rock to give the appointed signal to Coomara, which was throwing a big stone into the water. Jack threw, and up sprang Coo!

"Good morning, Jack," said he; "what do you want with me?"

"Just nothing at all to speak about, sir," returned Jack, "only to come and take a bit of dinner with me, if I might make so free as to ask you, and sure I'm now after doing so."

"It's quite agreeable, Jack, I assure you; what's your hour?"

"Any time that's most convenient to you, sir—say one o'clock, that you may go home, if you wish, with the daylight."

"I'll be with you," said Coo, "never fear me."

Jack went home, and dressed a noble fish dinner, and got out plenty of his best foreign spirits, enough, for that matter, to make twenty men drunk. Just to the minute came Coo, with his cocked hat under his arm. Dinner was ready, they sat down, and ate and drank away manfully. Jack, thinking of the poor souls below in the pots, plied old Coo well with brandy, and encouraged him to sing, hoping to put him under the table, but poor Jack forgot that he had not the sea over his head to keep it cool. The brandy got into it, and did his business for him, and Coo reeled off home, leaving his entertainer as dumb as a haddock on a Good Friday.

Jack never woke till the next morning, and then he was in a sad way. "'Tis to no use for me thinking to make that old rapparee drunk," said Jack, "and how in this world can I help the poor souls out of the lobster-pots?" After ruminating nearly the whole day, a thought struck him. "I have it," says he, slapping his knee; "I'll be sworn that Coo never saw a drop of poteen, as old as

he is, and that's the *thing* to settle him! Oh! then, is not it well that Biddy will not be home these two days yet; I can have another twist at him."

Jack asked Coo again, and Coo laughed at him for having no better head, telling him he'd never come up to his grandfather.

"Well, but try me again," said Jack, "and I'll be bail to drink you drunk and sober, and drunk again."

"Anything in my power," said Coo, "to oblige you."

At this dinner Jack took care to have his own liquor well watered, and to give the strongest brandy he had to Coo. At last says he, "Pray, sir, did you ever drink any poteen?—any real mountain dew?"

"No," says Coo; "what's that, and where does it come from?"

"Oh, that's a secret," said Jack, "but it's the right stuff—never believe me again, if 'tis not fifty times as good as brandy or rum either. Biddy's brother just sent me a present of a little drop, in exchange for some brandy, and as you're an old friend of the family, I kept it to treat you with."

"Well, let's see what sort of thing it is," said Coomara.

The poteen was the right sort. It was first-rate, and had the real smack upon it. Coo was delighted; he drank and he sung *Rum bum boodle boo* over and over again; and he laughed and he danced, till he fell on the floor fast asleep. Then Jack, who had taken good care to keep himself sober, snapt up the cocked hat—ran off to the rock—leaped in, and soon arrived at Coo's habitation.

All was as still as a churchyard at midnight—not a Merrow, old or young, was there. In he went and turned up the pots, but nothing did he see, only he heard a sort of a little whistle or chirp as he raised each of them. At this he was surprised, till he recollected what the priest had often said, that nobody living could see the soul, no more than they could see the wind or the air. Having now done all that he could for them, he set the pots as they were before, and sent a blessing after the poor souls to speed them on their journey wherever they were going. Jack now began to think of returning; he put the hat on, as was right, the wrong way; but when he got out he found the water so high over his head that he had no hopes of ever getting up into it, now that he had not old Coomara to give him a lift. He walked about looking for a ladder, but not one could be find, and not a rock was there in sight. At last he saw a spot where the sea hung rather lower than anywhere else, so he resolved to try there. Just as he came to it, a big cod happened to put down his tail. Jack made a jump and caught hold of it, and the cod, all in amazement, gave a bounce and pulled Jack up. The minute the hat touched the water away Jack was whisked, and up he shot like a cork, dragging the poor cod, that he forgot to let go, up with him tail foremost. He got to the rock in no time, and without a moment's delay hurried home, rejoicing in the good deed he had done.

But, meanwhile, there was fine work at home; for our friend Jack had hardly left the house on his soul-freeing expedition, when back came Biddy from her soul-saving one to the well. When she entered the house and saw the things lying *thrie-na-helah* on the table before her—"Here's a pretty job!" said she; "that blackguard of mine—what ill-luck I had ever to marry him! He has picked up some vagabond or other, while I was praying for the good of his soul, and they've been drinking all the poteen that my own brother gave him, and all the spirits, to be sure, that he was to have sold to his honour." Then hearing an outlandish kind of grunt, she looked down, and saw Coomara lying under the table. "The Blessed Virgin help me," shouted she, "if he has not made a real beast of himself! Well, well, I've often heard of a man making a beast of himself with drink! Oh hone, oh hone!—Jack, honey, what will I do with you, or what will I do without you? How can any decent woman ever think of living with a beast?"

With such like lamentations Biddy rushed out of the house, and was going she knew not where, when she heard the well-known voice of Jack singing a merry tune. Glad enough was Biddy to find him safe and sound, and not turned into a thing that was like neither fish nor flesh. Jack was obliged to tell her all, and Biddy, though she had half a mind to be angry with him for not telling her before, owned that he had done a great service to the poor souls. Back they both went most lovingly to the house, and Jack wakened up Coomara; and, perceiving the old fellow to be rather dull, he bid him not to be cast down, for 'twas many a good man's case; said it all came of his not being used to the poteen, and recommended him, by way of cure, to swallow a hair of the dog that bit him. Coo, however, seemed to think he had had quite enough. He got up, quite out of sorts, and without having the manners to say one word in the way of civility, he sneaked off to cool himself by a jaunt through the salt water.

Coomara never missed the souls. He and Jack continued the best friends in the world, and no one, perhaps, ever equalled Jack for freeing souls from purgatory; for he contrived fifty excuses for getting into the house below the sea, unknown to the old fellow, and then turning up the pots and letting out the souls. It vexed him, to be sure, that he could never see them; but as he knew the thing to be impossible, he was obliged to be satisfied.

Their intercourse continued for several years. However, one morning, on Jack's throwing in a stone as usual, he got no answer. He flung another, and another, still there was no reply. He went away, and returned the following morning, but it was to no purpose. As he was without the hat, he could not go down to see what had become of old Coo, but his belief was that the old man, or the old fish, or whatever he was—had either died, or had removed from that part of the country.

THE STOLEN BRIDE

Lady Wilde

∽

About the year 1670 there was a fine young fellow living at a place called Querin, in the County Clare. He was brave and strong and rich, for he had his own land and his own house, and not one to lord it over him. He was called the Kern of Querin. And many a time he would go out alone to shoot the wild fowl at night along the lonely strand and sometimes cross over northward to the broad east strand, about two miles away, to find the wild geese.

One cold frosty November Eve he was watching for them, crouched down behind the ruins of an old hut, when a loud splashing noise attracted his attention. It is the wild geese, he thought and, raising his gun, waited in death-like silence for the approach of his victim.

But presently he saw a dark mass moving along the edge of the strand. And he knew there were no wild geese near him. So he watched and waited till the black mass came closer, and then he distinctly perceived four stout men carrying a bier on their shoulders, on which lay a corpse covered with a white cloth. For a few moments they laid it down, apparently to rest themselves, and the Kern instantly fired; on which the four men ran away shrieking, and the corpse was left alone on the bier. Kern of Querin immediately sprang to the place, and lifting the cloth from the face of the corpse, beheld by the freezing starlight the form of a beautiful young girl, apparently not dead but in a deep sleep.

Gently he passed his hand over her face and raised her up, when she opened her eyes and looked around with wild wonder, but spake never a word, though he tried to soothe and encourage her. Then, thinking it was dangerous for them to remain in that place, he raised her from the bier, and taking her hand led her away to his own house. They arrived safely, but in silence. And for twelve months did she remain with the Kern, never tasting food or speaking word for all that time.

When the next November Eve came round, he resolved to visit the east strand again, and watch from the same place, in the hope of meeting with some adventure that might throw light on the history of the beautiful girl. His way lay beside the old ruined fort called Lios-na-faillainge (the Fort of the Mantle), and as he passed, the sound of music and mirth fell on his ear. He stopped to catch the words of the voices, and had not waited long when he heard a man say in a low whisper—"Where shall we go tonight to carry off a bride?"

And a second voice answered—"Wherever we go I hope better luck will be ours than we had this day twelvemonth."

"Yes," said a third; "on that night we carried off a rich prize, the fair daughter of O'Connor; but that clown, the Kern of Querin, broke our spell and took her from us. Yet little pleasure has he had of his bride, for she has neither eaten or drank nor uttered a word since she entered his house."

"And so she will remain," said a fourth, "until he makes her eat off her father's table-cloth, which covered her as she lay on the bier, and which is now thrown up over the top of her bed."

On hearing all this, the Kern rushed home and, without waiting even for the morning, entered the young girl's room, took down the table-cloth, spread it on the table, laid meat and drink thereon, and led her to it. "Drink," he said, "that speech may come to you." And she drank, and ate of the food, and then speech came. And she told the Kern her story—how she was to have been married to a young lord of her own country, and the wedding guests had all assembled, when she felt herself suddenly ill and swooned away, and never knew more of what had happened to her until the Kern had passed his hand over her face, by which she recovered consciousness but could neither eat nor speak, for a spell was on her, and she was helpless.

Then the Kern prepared a chariot, and carried home the young girl to her father, who was like to die for joy when he beheld her. And the Kern grew mightily in O'Connor's favour, so that at last he gave him his fair young daughter to wife; and the wedded pair lived together happily for many long years after, and no evil befell them, but good followed all the work of their hands.

This story of Kern of Querin still lingers in the faithful, vivid Irish memory, and is often told by the peasants of Clare when they gather round the fire on the awful festival of Samhain, or November Eve, when the dead walk and the spirits of earth and air have power over mortals, whether for good or evil.

THE SILKIE WIFE

Patrick Kennedy

~

Those that live in the Shetland and Orkney islands who know no better, are persuaded that the seals, or silkies, as they call them, can doss their coverings at times, and disport themselves as men and women. A fisher once turning a ridge of rock discovered a beautiful bit of green turf adjoining the shingle sheltered by rocks on the landward side, and over this turf and shingle two beautiful women chasing each other. Just at the man's feet lay two sealskins, one of which he took up to examine it. The women, catching sight of him, screamed out, and ran to get possession of the skins. One seized the article on the ground, donned it in a thrice, and plunged into the sea; the other wrung her hands, cried, and begged the fisher to restore her property; but he wanted a wife, and would not throw away the chance. He wooed her so earnestly and lovingly, that she put on some women's clothing which he brought her from his cottage, followed him home, and became his wife.

Some years later, when their home was enlivened by the presence of two children, the husband, awakening one night, heard voices in conversation from the kitchen. Stealing softly to the room door, he heard his wife talking in

a low tone with someone outside the window. The interview was just at an end, and he had only time to ensconce himself in bed, when his wife was stealing across the room. He was greatly disturbed, but determined to do or say nothing till he should acquire further knowledge.

Next evening, as he was returning home by the strand, he spied a male and female *phoca* sprawling on a rock a few yards out at sea. The rougher animal, raising himself on his tail and fins, thus addressed the astonished man in the dialect spoken in these islands:

"You deprived me of her whom I was to make my companion; and it was only yesterday that I discovered her outer garment, the loss of which obliged her to be your wife. I bear no malice as you were kind to her in your own fashion. Besides, my heart is too full of joy to hold any malice. Look on your wife for the last time."

The other seal glanced to him with all the shyness and sorrow she could force into her now uncouth features; but when the bereaved husband rushed towards the rock to secure his lost treasure, she and her companion were in the water on the other side of it in a moment, and the poor fisherman was obliged to return sadly to his motherless children and desolate home.

THE BRIDE'S DEATH SONG

Lady Wilde

⁓

On a lone island by the west coast there dwelt an old fisherman and his daughter, and the man had power over the water spirits, and he taught his daughter the charms that bind them to obey.

One day a boat was driven on the shore, and in it was a young, handsome gentleman, half dead from the cold and wet. The old fisherman brought him home and revived him, and Eileen, the daughter, nursed and watched him. Naturally the two young people soon fell in love, and the gentleman told the girl he had a beautiful house on the mainland ready for her, with plenty of everything she could desire—silks to wear and gold to spend. So they were betrothed, and the wedding day was fixed. But Dermot, the lover, said he must first cross to the mainland and bring back his friends and relations to the wedding, as many as the boat would hold.

Eileen wept and prayed him not to leave, or at least to take her to steer the boat, for she knew there was danger coming, and she alone could have power over the evil spirits and over the waves and the winds. But she dared not tell the secret of the spell to Dermot or it would fail, and the charm be useless for ever after.

Dermot, however, only laughed at her fears, for the day was bright and clear, and he scorned all thought of danger. So he put off from the shore, and reached the mainland safely, and filled the boat with his friends to return to the island for the wedding. All went well till they were within sight of the island, when suddenly a fierce gust of wind drove the boat on a rock, and it was upset, and all who were in it perished.

Eileen heard the cry of the drowning men as she stood watching on the beach, but could give no help. And she was sore grieved for her lover, and sang a funeral wail for him in Irish, which is still preserved by the people. Then she lay down and died, and the old man, her father, disappeared. And from that day no one has ever ventured to live on the island, for it is haunted by the spirit of Eileen. And the mournful music of her wail is still heard in the nights when the winds are strong and the waves beat upon the rocks where the drowned men lay dead.

The words of the song are very plaintive and simple, and may be translated literally:

I a virgin and a widow mourn for my lover.
Never more will he kiss me on the lips;
The cold wave is his bridal bed,
The cold wave is his wedding shroud.
O love, my love, had you brought me in the boat
My spirit and my spells would have saved from harm.
For my power was strong over waves and wind,
And the spirits of evil would have feared me.
O love, my love, I go to meet you in heaven.
I will ask God to let me see your face.
If the fair angels give me back my lover,
I will not envy the Almighty on His throne.

THE LEGEND OF KNOCKGRAFTON

T. Crofton Croker

~

There was once a poor man who lived in the fertile glen of Aherlow, at the foot of the gloomy Galtee mountains, and he had a great hump on his back: he looked just as if his body had been rolled up and placed upon his shoulders; and his head was pressed down with the weight so much that his chin, when he was sitting, used to rest upon his knees for support. The country people were rather shy of meeting him in any lonesome place, for though, poor creature, he was as harmless and as inoffensive as a new-born infant, yet his deformity was so great that he scarcely appeared to be a human creature, and some ill-minded persons had set strange stories about him afloat. He was said to have a great knowledge of herbs and charms; but certain it was that he had a mighty skillful hand in plaiting straws and rushes into hats and baskets, which was the way he made his livelihood.

Lusmore, for that was the nickname put upon him by reason of his always wearing a sprig of the fairy cap, or lusmore (the foxglove), in his little straw hat, would ever get a higher penny for his plaited work than any one else and perhaps that was the reason why some one, out of envy, had circulated the strange stories about him. Be that as it may, it happened that he was returning one evening from the pretty town of Cahir towards Cappagh, and as little Lusmore walked very slowly, on account of the great hump upon his back, it was quite dark when he came to the old moat of Knockgrafton, which stood on the right-hand side of his road. Tired and weary was he, and noways comfortable in his own mind at thinking how much farther he had to travel, and that he should be walking all the night; so he sat down under the moat to rest himself, and began looking mournfully enough upon the moon, which

> "Rising in clouded majesty, at length
> Apparent Queen, unveil'd her peerless light,
> And o'er the dark her silver mantle threw."

Presently there rose a wild strain of unearthly melody upon the ear of little Lusmore; he listened, and he thought that he had never heard such ravishing music before. It was like the sound of many voices, each mingling and blending with the other so strangely that they seemed to be one, though all singing different strains, and the words of the song were these:

> *Da Luan, Da Mort, Da Luan, Da Mort, Da Luan, Da Mort;*

when there would be a moment's pause, and then the round of melody went on again.

Lusmore listened attentively, scarcely drawing his breath lest he might lose the slightest note. He now plainly perceived that the singing was within the moat; and though at first it had charmed him so much, he began to get tired of hearing the same round sung over and over so often without any change; so availing himself of the pause when *Da Luan, Da Mort,* had been sung three times, he took up the tune, and raised it with the words *augus Da Dardeen,* and then went on singing with the voices inside of the moat, *Da Luan, Da Mort,* finishing the melody, when the pause again came, with *augus Da Dardeen.*

The fairies within Knockgrafton, for the song was a fairy melody, when they heard this addition to the tune, were so much delighted that, with instant resolve, it was determined to bring the mortal among them, whose musical skill so far exceeded theirs, and little Lusmore was conveyed into their company with the eddying speed of a whirlwind.

Glorious to behold was the sight that burst upon him as he came down through the moat, twirling round and round, with the lightness of a straw, to the sweetest music that kept time to his motion. The greatest honour was then paid him, for he was put above all the musicians, and he had servants tending upon him, and everything to his heart's content, and a hearty welcome to all; and, in short, he was made as much of as if he had been the first man in the land.

Presently Lusmore saw a great consultation going forward among the fairies, and, notwithstanding all their civility, he felt very much frightened, until one stepping out from the rest came up to him and said:

> "Lusmore! Lusmore!
> Doubt not, nor deplore,
> For the hump which you bore
> On your back is no more;
> Look down on the floor,
> And view it, Lusmore!"

When these words were said, poor little Lusmore felt himself so light, and so happy, that he thought he could have bounded at one jump over the moon, like the cow in the history of the cat and the fiddle; and he saw, with inexpressible pleasure, his hump tumble down upon the ground from his shoulders. He then tried to lift up his head, and he did so with becoming caution, fearing that he might knock it against the ceiling of the grand hall, where he was; he looked round and round again with the greatest wonder and delight upon everything, which appeared more and more beautiful; and, overpowered at beholding such a resplendent scene, his head grew dizzy, and his eyesight became dim. At last he fell into a sound sleep, and when he awoke he found that it was broad daylight, the sun shining brightly, and the birds singing sweetly; and that he was lying just at the foot of the moat of Knockgrafton, with the cows and sheep grazing peaceably round about him. The first thing Lusmore did, after saying his prayers, was to put his hand behind to feel for his hump, but no sign of one was there on his back, and he looked at himself with great pride, for he had now become a well-shaped dapper little fellow, and more than that, found himself in a full suit of new clothes, which he concluded the fairies had made for him.

Towards Cappagh he went, stepping out as lightly, and springing up at every step as if he had been all his life a dancing-master. Not a creature who met Lusmore knew him without his hump, and he had a great work to persuade every one that he was the same man—in truth he was not, so far as the outward appearance went.

Of course it was not long before the story of Lusmore's hump got about, and a great wonder was made of it. Through the country, for miles round, it was the talk of every one, high and low.

One morning, as Lusmore was sitting contented enough at his cabin door, up came an old woman to him, and asked him if he could direct her to Cappagh.

"I need give you no directions, my good woman," said Lusmore, "for this is Cappagh; and whom may you want here?"

"I have come," said the woman, "out of Decie's country, in the county of Waterford, looking after one Lusmore, who, I have heard tell, had his hump taken off by the fairies; for there is a son of a gossip of mine who has got a hump on him that will be his death; and maybe, if he could use the same charm as Lusmore, the hump may be taken off him. And now I have told you the reason of my coming so far: 'tis to find out about this charm, if I can."

Lusmore, who was ever a good-natured little fellow, told the woman all the particulars, how he had raised the tune for the fairies at Knockgrafton, how his hump had been removed from his shoulders, and how he had got a new suit of clothes into the bargain.

The woman thanked him very much, and then went away quite happy and easy in her mind. When she came back to her gossip's house, in the county of Waterford, she told her everything that Lusmore had said, and they put the little hump-backed man, who was a peevish and cunning creature from his birth, upon a car, and took him all the way across the country. It was a long journey, but they did not care for that, so the hump was taken from off him; and they brought him, just at nightfall, and left him under the old moat of Knockgrafton.

Jack Madden, for that was the humpy man's name, had not been sitting there long when he heard the tune going on within the moat much sweeter than before; for the fairies were singing it the way Lusmore had settled their music for them, and the song was going on: *Da Luan, Da Mort, Da Luan, Da*

Mort, Da Luan, Da Mort, augus Da Dardeen, without ever stopping. Jack Madden, who was in a great hurry to get quit of his hump, never thought of waiting until the fairies had done, or watching for a fit opportunity to raise the tune higher again than Lusmore had; so having heard them sing it over seven times without stopping, out he bawls, never minding the time or the humour of the tune, or how he could bring his words in properly, *augus Da Dardeen, augus Da Hena,* thinking that if one day was good, two were better; and that if Lusmore had one new suit of clothes given him, he should have two.

No sooner had the words passed his lips than he was taken up and whisked into the moat with prodigious force; and the fairies came crowding round about him with great anger, screeching and screaming, and roaring out:

"Who spoiled our tune? Who spoiled our tune?" and one stepped up to him above all the rest, and said:

> "Jack Madden! Jack Madden!
> Your words came so bad in
> The tune we felt glad in;—
> This castle you're had in,
> That your life we may sadden;
> Here's two humps for Jack Madden!"

And twenty of the strongest fairies brought Lusmore's hump, and put it down upon poor Jack's back, over his own, where it became fixed as firmly as if it was nailed on with twelve-penny nails, by the best carpenter that ever drove one. Out of their castle they then kicked him; and in the morning, when Jack Madden's mother and her gossip came to look after their little man, they found him half dead, lying at the foot of the moat, with the other hump upon his back. Well to be sure, how they did look at each other! but they were afraid to say anything, lest a hump might be put upon their own shoulders. Home they brought the unlucky Jack Madden with them, as downcast in their hearts and their looks as ever two gossips were; and what through the weight of his other hump, and the long journey, he died soon after, leaving, they say, his heavy curse to any one who would go to listen to fairy tunes again.

TEIG O'KANE AND
THE CORPSE

Douglas Hyde

~

There was once a grown-up lad in the county Leitrim, and he was
strong and lively, and the son of a rich farmer. His father had plenty of money,
and he did not spare it on the son. Accordingly, when the boy grew up he liked
sport better than work, and, as his father had no other children, he loved this
one so much that he allowed him to do in everything just as it pleased himself.
He was very extravagant, and he used to scatter the gold money as another
person would scatter the white. He was seldom to be found at home, but if
there was a fair, or a race, or a gathering within ten miles of him, you were
dead certain to find him there. And he seldom spent a night in his father's
house, but he used to be always out rambling, and, like Shawn Bwee long ago,
there was

"grádh gach cailin i mbrollach a léine,"

"the love of every girl in the breast of his shirt," and it's manys the kiss he got
and he gave, for he was very handsome, and there wasn't a girl in the country

but would fall in love with him, only for him to fasten his two eyes on her, and it was for that someone made this *rann* on him—

"Feuch an rógaire 'g iarraidh póige,
Ni h-iongantas mór é a bheith mar atá
Ag leanamhaint a gcómhnuidhe d'árnán na gráineóige
Anuas 's anios 's nna chodladh 'sa' lá."

i.e.—

"Look at the rogue, it's for kisses he's rambling.
It isn't much wonder, for that was his way;
He's like an old hedgehog, at night he'll be scrambling
From this place to that, but he'll sleep in the day."

At last he became very wild and unruly. He wasn't to be seen day nor night in his father's house, but always rambling or going on his *kailee* (night-visit) from place to place and from house to house, so that the old people used to shake their heads and say to one another, "It's easy seen what will happen to the land when the old man dies; his son will run through it in a year, and it won't stand him that long itself."

He used to be always gambling and card-playing and drinking, but his father never minded his bad habits, and never punished him. But it happened one day that the old man was told that the son had ruined the character of a girl in the neighbourhood, and he was greatly angry, and he called the son to him, and said to him, quietly and sensibly—"Avic," says he, "you know I loved you greatly up to this, and I never stopped you from doing your choice thing whatever it was, and I kept plenty of money with you, and I always hoped to leave you the house and land, and all I had after myself would be gone; but I heard a story of you to-day that has disgusted me with you. I cannot tell you the grief that I felt when I heard such a thing of you, and I tell you now plainly that unless you marry that girl I'll leave house and land and everything to my brother's son. I never could leave it to anyone who would make so bad a use of it as you do yourself, deceiving women and coaxing girls. Settle with yourself now whether you'll marry that girl and get my land as a fortune with her, or refuse to marry her and give up all that was coming to you; and tell me in the morning which of the two things you have chosen."

"Och! *Domnoo Sheery!* father, you wouldn't say that to me, and I such a good son as I am. Who told you I wouldn't marry the girl?" says he.

But his father was gone, and the lad knew well enough that he would keep his word too; and he was greatly troubled in his mind, for as quiet and as kind as the father was, he never went back of a word that he had once said, and there wasn't another man in the country who was harder to bend than he was.

The boy did not know rightly what to do. He was in love with the girl indeed, and he hoped to marry her some time or other, but he would much sooner have remained another while as he was, and follow on at his old tricks—drinking, sporting, and playing cards; and, along with that, he was angry that his father should order him to marry, and should threaten him if he did not do it.

"Isn't my father a great fool!" says he to himself. "I was ready enough, and only too anxious, to marry Mary; and now since he threatened me, faith I've a great mind to let it go another while."

His mind was so much excited that he remained between two notions as to what he should do. He walked out into the night at last to cool his heated blood, and went on to the road. He lit a pipe, and as the night was fine he walked and walked on, until the quick pace made him begin to forget his trouble. The night was bright, and the moon half full. There was not a breath of wind blowing, and the air was calm and mild. He walked on for nearly three hours, when he suddenly remembered that it was late in the night, and time for him to turn. "Musha! I think I forgot myself," says he; "it must be near twelve o'clock now."

The word was hardly out of his mouth, when he heard the sound of many

voices, and the trampling of feet on the road before him. "I don't know who can be out so late at night as this, and on such a lonely road," said he to himself.

He stood listening, and he heard the voices of many people talking through other[*sic*], but he could not understand what they were saying. "Oh, wirra!" says he, "I'm afraid. It's not Irish or English they have; it can't be they're Frenchmen!" He went on a couple of yards farther, and he saw well enough by the light of the moon a band of little people coming towards him, and they were carrying something big and heavy with them.

"Oh, murder!" says he to himself, "sure it can't be that they're the good people that's in it!" Every *rib* of hair that was on his head stood up, and there fell a shaking on his bones, for he saw that they were coming to him fast.

He looked at them again, and perceived that there were about twenty little men in it, and there was not a man at all of them higher than about three feet or three feet and a half, and some of them were grey, and seemed very old. He looked again, but he could not make out what was the heavy thing they were carrying until they came up to him, and then they all stood round about him. They threw the heavy thing down on the road, and he saw on the spot that it was a dead body.

He became as cold as the Death, and there was not a drop of blood running in his veins when an old little grey *maneen* came up to him and said, "Isn't it lucky we met you, Teig O'Kane?"

Poor Teig could not bring out a word at all, nor open his lips, if he were to get the word for it, and so he gave no answer.

"Teig O'Kane," said the little grey man again, "isn't it timely you met us?"

Teig could not answer him.

"Teig O'Kane," says he, "the third time, isn't it lucky and timely that we met you?"

But Teig remained silent, for he was afraid to return an answer, and his tongue was as if it was tied to the roof of his mouth.

The little grey man turned to his companions, and there was joy in his bright little eye. "And now," says he, "Teig O'Kane hasn't a word, we can do with him what we please. Teig, Teig," says he, "you're living a bad life, and we can make a slave of you now, and you cannot withstand us, for there's no use in trying to go against us. Lift that corpse."

Teig was so frightened that he was only able to utter the two words, "I won't"; for as frightened as he was, he was obstinate and stiff, the same as ever.

"Teig O'Kane won't lift the corpse," said the little *maneen,* with a wicked little laugh, for all the world like the breaking of a *lock* of dry *kippens,* and with a little harsh voice like the striking of a cracked bell. "Teig O'Kane won't lift the corpse—make him lift it"; and before the word was out of his mouth they had all gathered round poor Teig, and they all talking and laughing through other.

Teig tried to run from them, but they followed him, and a man of them stretched out his foot before him as he ran, so that Teig was thrown in a heap on the road. Then before he could rise up the fairies caught him, some by the hands and some by the feet, and they held him tight, in a way that he could not stir, with his face against the ground. Six or seven of them raised the body then, and pulled it over to him, and left it down on his back. The breast of the corpse was squeezed against Teig's back and shoulders, and the arms of the corpse were thrown around Teig's neck. Then they stood back from him a couple of yards, and let him get up. He rose, foaming at the mouth and cursing, and he shook himself, thinking to throw the corpse off his back. But his fear and his wonder were great when he found that the two arms had a tight hold round his own neck, and that the two legs were squeezing his hips firmly, and that, however strongly he tried, he could not throw it off, any more than a horse can throw off its saddle. He was terribly frightened then, and he thought he was lost. "Ochone! for ever," said he to himself, "it's the bad life I'm leading that has given the good people this power over me. I promise to God and Mary, Peter and Paul, Patrick and Bridget, that I'll mend my ways for as long as I have to live, if I come clear out of this danger—and I'll marry the girl."

The little grey man came up to him again, and said he to him, "Now, Teig*een*," says he, "you didn't lift the body when I told you to lift it, and see how you were made to lift it; perhaps when I tell you to bury it you won't bury it until you're made to bury it!"

"Anything at all that I can do for your honour," said Teig, "I'll do it," for he was getting sense already, and if it had not been for the great fear that was on him, he never would have let that civil word slip out of his mouth.

The little man laughed a sort of laugh again. "You're getting quiet now, Teig," says he. "I'll go bail but you'll be quiet enough before I'm done with you. Listen to me now, Teig O'Kane, and if you don't obey me in all I'm telling you to do, you'll repent it. You must carry with you this corpse that is on your back to Teampoll-Démus, and you must bring it into the church with you, and make a grave for it in the very middle of the church, and you must raise up the flags and put them down again the very same way, and you must carry the clay out of the church and leave the place as it was when you came, so that no one could know that there had been anything changed. But that's not all. Maybe that the body won't be allowed to be buried in the church; perhaps some other man has the bed, and, if so, it's likely he won't share it with this one. If you don't get leave to bury it in Teampoll-Démus, you must carry it to Carrick-fhad-vic-Orus, and bury it in the churchyard there; and if you don't get into that place, take it with you to Teampoll-Ronan; and if that churchyard is closed on you, take it to Imlogue-Fada; and if you're not able to bury it there, you've no more to do than to take it to Kill-Breedya, and you can bury it there without hindrance. I cannot tell you what one of those churches is the one where you will have leave to bury that corpse under the clay, but I know that it will be allowed you to bury him at some church or other of them. If you do this work rightly, we will be thankful to you, and you will have no cause to grieve; but if you are slow or lazy, believe me we shall take satisfaction of you."

When the grey little man had done speaking, his comrades laughed and clapped their hands together. "Glic! Glic! Hwee! Hwee!" they all cried; "go on, go on, you have eight hours before you till daybreak, and if you haven't this man buried before the sun rises, you're lost." They struck a fist and a foot behind on him, and drove him on in the road. He was obliged to walk, and to walk fast, for they gave him no rest.

He thought himself that there was not a wet path, or a dirty *boreen,* or a crooked contrary road in the whole county, that he had not walked that night. The night was at times very dark, and whenever there would come a cloud across the moon he could see nothing, and then he used often to fall. Sometimes he was hurt, and sometimes he escaped, but he was obliged always to rise on the moment and to hurry on. Sometimes the moon would break out clearly, and then he would look behind him and see the little people following his back. And he heard them speaking amongst themselves, talking and crying out, and screaming like a flock of sea-gulls; and if he was to save his soul he never understood as much as one word of what they were saying.

He did not know how far he had walked, when at last one of them cried out to him, "Stop here!" He stood, and they all gathered round him.

"Do you see those withered trees over there?" says the old boy to him again. "Teampoll-Démus is among those trees, and you must go in there by yourself, for we cannot follow you or go with you. We must remain here. Go on boldly."

Teig looked from him, and he saw a high wall that was in places half broken down, and an old grey church on the inside of the wall, and about a dozen withered old trees scattered here and there around it. There was neither leaf nor twig on any of them, but their bare crooked branches were stretched out like the arms of an angry man when he threatens. He had no help for it, but was obliged to go forward. He was a couple of hundred yards from the church, but he walked on, and never looked behind him until he came to the gate of the churchyard. The old gate was thrown down, and he had no difficulty in entering. He turned then to see if any of the little people were following him, but there came a cloud over the moon, and the night became so dark that he could see nothing. He went into the churchyard, and he walked up the old

grassy pathway leading to the church. When he reached the door, he found it locked. The door was large and strong, and he did not know what to do. At last he drew out his knife with difficulty, and stuck it in the wood to try if it were not rotten, but it was not.

"Now," said he to himself, "I have no more to do; the door is shut, and I can't open it."

Before the words were rightly shaped in his own mind, a voice in his ear said to him, "Search for the key on the top of the door, or on the wall."

He started. "Who is that speaking to me?" he cried, turning round; but he saw no one. The voice said in his ear again, "Search for the key on the top of the door, or on the wall."

"What's that?" said he, and the sweat running from his forehead; "who spoke to me?"

"It's I, the corpse, that spoke to you!" said the voice.

"Can you talk?" said Teig.

"Now and again," said the corpse.

Teig searched for the key, and he found it on the top of the wall. He was too much frightened to say any more, but he opened the door wide, and as quickly as he could, and he went in, with the corpse on his back. It was as dark as pitch inside, and poor Teig began to shake and tremble.

"Light the candle," said the corpse.

Teig put his hand in his pocket, as well as he was able, and drew out a flint and steel. He struck a spark out of it, and lit a burnt rag he had in his pocket. He blew it until it made a flame, and he looked round him. The church was very ancient, and part of the wall was broken down. The windows were blown in or cracked, and the timber of the seats was rotten. There were six or seven old iron candlesticks left there still, and in one of these candlesticks Teig found the stump of an old candle, and he lit it. He was still looking round him on the strange and horrid place in which he found himself, when the cold corpse whispered in his ear, "Bury me now, bury me now; there is a spade and turn the ground." Teig looked from him, and he saw a spade lying beside the altar. He took it up, and he placed the blade under a flag that was in the middle of the aisle, and leaning all his weight on the handle of the spade, he raised it. When the first flag was raised it was not hard to raise the others near it, and he moved three or four of them out of their places. The clay that was under them was soft and easy to dig, but he had not thrown up more than three or four shovelfuls, when he felt the iron touch something soft like flesh. He threw up three or four more shovelfuls from around it, and then he saw that it was another body that was buried in the same place.

"I am afraid I'll never be allowed to bury the two bodies in the same hole," said Teig, in his own mind. "You corpse, there on my back," says he, "will you be satisfied if I bury you down here?" But the corpse never answered him a word.

"That's a good sign," said Teig to himself. "Maybe he's getting quiet," and he thrust the spade down in the earth again. Perhaps he hurt the flesh of the other body, for the dead man that was buried there stood up in the grave, and shouted an awful shout. "Hoo! hoo!! hoo!!! Go! go!! go!!! or you're a dead, dead, dead man!" And then he fell back in the grave again. Teig said afterwards, that of all the wonderful things he saw that night, that was the most awful to him. His hair stood upright on his head like the bristles of a pig, the cold sweat ran off his face, and then came a tremor over all his bones, until he thought that he must fall.

But after a while he became bolder, when he saw that the second corpse remained lying quietly there, and he threw in the clay on it again, and he smoothed it overhead, and he laid down the flags carefully as they had been before. "It can't be that he'll rise up any more," said he.

He went down the aisle a little farther, and drew near to the door, and began raising the flags again, looking for another bed for the corpse on his back. He took up three or four flags and put them aside, and then he dug the clay. He was not long digging until he laid bare an old woman without a thread upon her but her shirt. She was more lively than the first corpse, for he had scarcely taken any of the clay away from about her, when she sat up and began to cry, "Ho, you *bodach* (clown)! Ha, you *bodach!* Where has he been that he got no bed?"

Poor Teig drew back, and when she found that she was getting no answer, she closed her eyes gently, lost her vigour, and fell back quietly and slowly under the clay. Teig did to her as he had done to the man—he threw the clay back on her, and left the flags down overhead.

He began digging again near the door, but before he had thrown up more than a couple of shovelfuls, he noticed a man's hand laid bare by the spade. "By my soul, I'll go no farther, then," said he to himself; "what use is it for me?" And he threw the clay in again on it, and settled the flags as they had been before.

He left the church then and his heart was heavy enough, but he shut the door and locked it, and left the key where he found it. He sat down on a tombstone that was near the door, and began thinking. He was in great doubt what he should do. He laid his face between his two hands, and cried for grief and fatigue, since he was dead certain at this time that he never would come home alive. He made another attempt to loosen the hands of the corpse that were squeezed round his neck, but they were as tight as if they were clamped; and the more he tried to loosen them, the tighter they squeezed him. He was going to sit down once more, when the cold, horrid lips of the dead man said to him, "Carrick-fhad-vic-Orus," and he remembered the command of the good people to bring the corpse with him to that place if he should be unable to bury it where he had been.

He rose up, and looked about him. "I don't know the way," he said.

As soon as he had uttered the word, the corpse stretched out suddenly its left hand that had been tightened round his neck, and kept it pointing out, showing him the road he ought to follow. Teig went in the direction that the fingers were stretched, and passed out of the churchyard. He found himself on an old rutty, stony road, and he stood still again, not knowing where to turn. The corpse stretched out its bony hand a second time, and pointed out to him another road—not the road by which he had come when approaching the old church. Teig followed that road, and whenever he came to a path or road meeting it, the corpse always stretched out its hand and pointed with its fingers, showing him the way he was to take.

Many was the cross-road he turned down, and many was the crooked *boreen* he walked, until he saw from him an old burying-ground at last, beside the road, but there was neither church nor chapel nor any other building in it. The corpse squeezed him tightly, and he stood. "Bury me, bury me in the burying-ground," said the voice.

Teig drew over towards the old burying-place, and he was not more than about twenty yards from it, when, raising his eyes, he saw hundreds and hundreds of ghosts—men, women, and children—sitting on the top of the wall round about, or standing on the inside of it, or running backwards and forwards, and pointing at him, while he could see their mouths opening and shutting as if they were speaking, though he heard no word, nor any sound amongst them at all.

He was afraid to go forward, so he stood where he was, and the moment he stood, all the ghosts became quiet, and ceased moving. Then Teig understood that it was trying to keep him from going in, that they were. He walked a couple of yards forwards, and immediately the whole crowd rushed together towards the spot to which he was moving, and they stood so thickly together that it seemed to him that he never could break through them, even though he had a mind to try. But he had no mind to try it. He went back broken and dispirited, and when he had gone a couple of hundred yards from the burying-ground, he stood again, for he did not know what way he was to go. He heard the voice of the corpse in his ear, saying "Teampoll-Ronan," and the skinny hand was stretched out again, pointing him out the road.

As tired as he was, he had to walk, and the road was neither short nor even. The night was darker than ever, and it was difficult to make his way. Many was the toss he got, and many a bruise they left on his body. At last he saw Teampoll-Ronan from him in the distance, standing in the middle of the burying-ground. He moved over towards it, and thought he was all right and safe, when he saw no ghosts nor anything else on the wall, and he thought he would never be hindered now from leaving his load off him at last. He moved over to the gate, but as he was passing in, he tripped on the threshold. Before he could recover himself, something that he could not see seized him by the neck, by the hands, and by the feet, and bruised him, and shook him, and choked him, until he was nearly dead; and at last he was lifted up, and carried more than a hundred yards from that place, and then thrown down in an old dyke, with the corpse still clinging to him.

He rose up, bruised and sore, but feared to go near the place again, for he had seen nothing the time he was thrown down and carried away.

"You corpse, up on my back," said he, "shall I go over again to the church-yard?"—but the corpse never answered him.

"That's a sign you don't wish me to try it again," said Teig.

He was now in great doubt as to what he ought to do, when the corpse spoke in his ear, and said, "Imlogue-Fada."

"Oh, murder!" said Teig, "must I bring you there? If you keep me long walking like this, I tell you I'll fall under you."

He went on, however, in the direction the corpse pointed out to him. He could not have told, himself, how long he had been going, when the dead man behind suddenly squeezed him, and said, "There!"

Teig looked from him, and he saw a little low wall, that was so broken down in places that it was no wall at all. It was in a great wide field, in from the road; and only for three or four great stones at the corners, that were more like rocks than stones, there was nothing to show that there was either grave-yard or burying-ground there.

"Is this Imlogue-Fada? Shall I bury you here?" said Teig.

"Yes," said the voice.

"But I see no grave or gravestone, only this pile of stones," said Teig.

The corpse did not answer, but stretched out its long fleshless hand, to show Teig the direction in which he was to go. Teig went on accordingly, but he was greatly terrified, for he remembered what had happened to him at the last place. He went on, "with his heart in his mouth," as he said himself after-wards; but when he came to within fifteen or twenty yards of the little low, square wall, there broke out a flash of lightning, bright yellow and red, with blue streaks in it, and went round about the wall in one course, and it swept by as fast as the swallow in the clouds, and the longer Teig remained looking at it the faster it went, till at last it became like a bright ring of flame round the old graveyard, which no one could pass without being burnt by it. Teig never saw, from the time he was born, and never saw afterwards, so wonderful or so splendid a sight as that was. Round went the flame, white and yellow and blue sparks leaping out from it as it went, and although at first it had been no more than a thin, narrow line, it increased slowly until it was at last a great broad band, and it was continually getting broader and higher, and throwing out more brilliant sparks, till there was never a colour on the ridge of the earth that was not to be seen in that fire; and lightning never shone and flame never flamed that was so shining and so bright as that.

Teig was amazed; he was half dead with fatigue, and he had no courage left to approach the wall. There fell a mist over his eyes, and there came a *soorawn* in his head, and he was obliged to sit down upon a great stone to recover himself. He could see nothing but the light, and he could hear nothing but the whirr of it as it shot round the paddock faster than a flash of lighting.

As he sat there on the stone, the voice whispered once more in his ear, "Kill-Breedya"; and the dead man squeezed him so tightly that he cried out. He rose again, sick, tired, and trembling, and went forwards as he was directed. The wind was cold, and the road was bad, and the load upon his back was heavy, and the night was dark, and he himself was nearly worn out, and if he had had very much farther to go he must have fallen dead under his burden.

At last the corpse stretched out its hand, and said to him, "Bury me there."

"This is the last burying-place," said Teig in his own mind; "and the little grey man said I'd be allowed to bury him in some of them, so it must be this; it can't be but they'll let him in here."

The first faint streak of the *ring of day* was appearing in the east, and the clouds were beginning to catch fire, but it was darker than ever, for the moon was set, and there were no stars.

"Make haste, make haste!" said the corpse; and Teig hurried forward as well as he could to the graveyard, which was a little place on a bare hill, with only a few graves in it.

He walked boldly in through the open gate, and nothing touched him, nor did he either hear or see anything. He came to the middle of the ground, and then stood up and looked round him for a spade or shovel to make a grave. As he was turning round and searching, he suddenly perceived what startled him greatly—a newly-dug grave right before him. He moved over to it, and looked down, and there at the bottom he saw a black coffin. He clambered down into the hole and lifted the lid, and found that (as he thought it would be) the coffin was empty. He had hardly mounted up out of the hole, and was standing on the brink, when the corpse, which had clung to him for more than eight hours, suddenly relaxed its hold of his neck, and loosened its shins from round his hips, and sank down with a *plop* into the open coffin.

Teig fell down on his two knees at the brink of the grave, and gave thanks to God. He made no delay then, but pressed down the coffin lid in its place, and threw in the clay over it with his two hands; and when the grave was filled up, he stamped and leaped on it with his feet, until it was firm and hard, and then he left the place.

The sun was fast rising as he finished his work and the first thing he did was to return to the road, and look out for a house to rest himself in. He found an inn at last, and lay down upon a bed there, and slept till night. Then he rose up and ate a little, and fell asleep again till morning. When he awoke in the morning he hired a horse and rode home. He was more than twenty-six miles from home where he was, and he had come all that way with the dead body on his back in one night.

All the people at his own home thought that he must have left the country, and they rejoiced greatly when they saw him come back. Everyone began asking him where he had been, but he would not tell anyone except his father.

He was a changed man from that day. He never drank too much; he never lost his money over cards; and especially he would not take the world and be out late by himself of a dark night.

He was not a fortnight at home until he married Mary, the girl he had been in love with; and it's at their wedding the sport was, and it's he was the happy man from that day forward, and it's all I wish that we may be as happy as he was.

THE FAIRY CHILD

Patrick Kennedy

~

*T*here was a sailor that lived up in Grange when he was at home, and one time, when he was away seven or eight months, his wife was brought to bed of a fine boy. She expected her husband back soon, and she wished to put off the christening of the child till he'd be on the spot. She and her husband were not natives of the country, and they were not as much afraid of leaving the child unchristened as our people would be.

Well, the child grew and throve, and the neighbours all bothered the woman to take him to Father M.'s to be baptised, and all they said was no use. "Her husband would be soon home, and then they'd have a joyful christening."

There happened to be no one sick up in that neighbourhood for some time, so the priest did not come to the place, nor hear of the birth, and none of the people about her could make up their minds to tell upon her, it is such an ugly thing to be informing; and then the child was so healthy, and the father might be on the spot any moment.

So the time crept on, and the lad was a year and a half old, and his mother up to that time never lost five nights' rest by him; when one evening that she came in from binding after the reapers, she heard wonderful whingeing and lamenting from the bed where he used to sleep. She ran over to him and asked him what ailed him. "Oh, mammy, I'm sick, and I'm hungry, and I'm cold, don't pull down the blanket." Well, the poor woman ran and got some boiled bread and milk as soon as she could, and asked her other son, that was about seven years old, when he took sick. "Oh, mother," says he, "he was happy as a king, playing near the fire about two hours ago, and I was below in the room, when I heard a great rush like as if a whole number of fowls were flying down the chimney. I heard my brother giving a great cry, and then another sound like as if the fowls were flying out again; when I got into the kitchen there he was, so miserable-looking and his clothes and his poor face so dirty. Take a look at him, and try do you know him at all."

So when she went to feed him she got such a fright, for his poor face was like an old man's and his body, and legs, and arms, all thin and hairy. But still he resembled the child she left in the morning, and "mammy, mammy" was never out of his mouth. She heard of people being fairy struck, so she supposed it was that that happened to him, but she never suspected her own child to be gone, and a fairy child left in its place.

Well, it's he that kept the poor woman awake many a night after, and never let her have a quiet day, crying for bread and milk, and mashed potatoes, and stirabout; and it was still "mammy, mammy, mammy," and the glows and the moans were never out of his mouth. Well, he had like to eat the poor woman out of house and home, and the very flesh off her bones with watching and sorrow. Still nothing could persuade her that it wasn't her own child that was in it.

One neighbour and another neighbour told her their minds plain enough. "Now, ma'am, you see what it is to leave a child without being christened. If you done your duty, fairy, nor spirit, nor divel, would have no power over your child. That *ounkran* in the bed is no more your child nor I am, but a little imp that the *Daoine Sidhe*—God between us and harm!—left you. By this and by that, if you don't whip him up and come along with us to Father M.'s, we'll go, hot foot, ourselves, and tell him all about it. Christened he must be before the day is older."

So she went over and soothered him, and said, "Come, *alanna*, let me dress you, and we'll go and be christened." And such roaring and screeching as came out of his throat would frighten the Danes. "I haven't the heart," says she at last, "and sure if we attempted to take him in that state we'd have the people of the three townlands following us to the priest's, and I'm afraid he'd take it very badly."

The next day when she came in, in the evening, she found him quite clean and fresh-looking, and his hair nicely combed. "Ah, Pat," says she to her other son, "was it you that done this?" Well, he said nothing till he and his mother were up at the fire, and the *angashore* of a child in his bed in the room. "Mother," says he then, in a whisper, "the neighbours are right, and you are wrong. I was out a little bit, and when I was coming round by the wall at the back of the room, I heard some sweet voices as if they were singing inside; and so I went to the crack in the corner, and what was round the bed but a whole parcel of nicely-dressed little women, with green gowns, and they singing, and dressing the little fellow, and combing his hair, and he laughing and crowing with them. I watched for a long time, and then stole round to the door, but the moment I pulled the string of the latch I heard the music change to his whimpering and crying, and when I got into the room there was no sign of anything only himself. He was a little better looking, but as cantankerous as ever."

"Ah," says the mother, "you are only joining the ill-natured neighbours. You're not telling a word of truth."

Next day Pat had a new story. "Mother," says he, "I was sitting here while you were out, and I began to wonder why he was so quiet, so I went into the room to see if he was asleep. There he was, sitting up with his old face on him, and he frightened the life out of me, he spoke so plain. '*Paudh*,' says he, 'go and light your mother's pipe, and let me have a shough; I'm tired o' my life lying here.' 'Ah, you thief' says I, 'wait till you hear what she'll say to you when I tell her this.' 'Tell away, you pick-thanks,' says he, 'she won't believe a word you say.' " "And neither do I believe one word from you," said the mother.

At last a letter came from the father, saying he'd be home after the letter as soon as coaches and ships could carry him. "Now," says the poor woman,

"we'll have the christening anyway." So the next day she went to New Ross to buy sugar and tay, and beef and pork, to give a grand let-out to welcome her husband, but bedad the long-headed neighbours took the opportunity to gain their ends of the fairy imp. They gathered round the house, and one stout woman came up to the bed, promiskis-like, and wrapped him up in the quilt before he had time to defend himself, and away down the lane to the Boro she went, and the whole townland at her heels. He thought to get away, but she held him pinned as if he was in a vice, and he kept roaring, and the crowd kept laughing, and they never crack-cried till they were at the stepping-stones going to Ballybawn from Grange.

Well, when he felt himself near the water he roared like a score of bulls, and kicked like the divel, but my brave woman wasn't to be daunted. She got on the first stepping-stone, and water, as black as night from the turf-mould running under her. He felt as heavy as lead, but she held on to the second. Well, she thought she'd go down there with the roaring, and the weight, and the dismal colour of the river, but she got to the middle stone, and there down through the quilt he fell as a heavy stone would through a muslin handkerchief. Off he went, whirling round and round, and letting the frightfulest laughs out of him, and showing his teeth and cracking his fingers at the people on the banks. "Oh, yous think yous are very clever, now," says he. "You may tell that fool of a woman from me that all I'm sorry for is that I didn't choke her, or do worse for her, before her husband comes home; bad luck to yous all!"

Well, they all came back joyful enough, though they were a little frightened. But weren't they rejoiced to meet the poor woman running to them with her fine healthy child in her arms, that she found in a delightful sleep when she got back from the town. You may be sure the next day didn't pass over him till he was baptised, and the next day his father got safe home. Well, I needn't say how happy they were; but bedad the woman was a little ashamed of herself next Sunday at Rathnure Chapel while Father James was preaching about the wickedness of neglecting to get young babies baptised as soon as possible after they're born.

A WOLF STORY

Lady Wilde

~

A young farmer, named Connor, once missed two fine cows from his herd, and no tale or tidings could be heard of them anywhere. So he thought he would set out on a search throughout the country; and he took a stout blackthorn stick in his hand, and went his way. All day he travelled miles and miles, but never a sign of the cattle. And the evening began to grow very dark, and he was wearied and hungry, and no place near to rest in; for he was in the midst of a bleak and desolate heath, with never a habitation at all in sight, except a long, low, rude sheiling, like the den of a robber or a wild beast. But a gleam of light came from a chink between the boards, and Connor took heart and went up and knocked at the door. It was opened at once by a tall, thin, grey-haired old man, with keen dark eyes.

"Come in," he said, "you are welcome. We have been waiting for you. This is my wife," and he brought him over to the hearth, where was seated an old thin, grey woman, with long sharp teeth and terrible glittering eyes.

"You are welcome," she said. "We have been waiting for you—it is time for supper. Sit down and eat with us."

Now Connor was a brave fellow, but he was a little dazed at first at the sight of this strange creature. However, as he had his stout stick with him, he thought he could make a fight for his life any way, and meantime, he would rest and eat, for he was both hungry and weary, and it was now black night, and he would never find his way home even if he tried. So he sat down by the hearth, while the old grey woman stirred the pot on the fire. But Connor felt that she was watching him all the time with her keen, sharp eyes.

Then a knock came to the door. And the old man rose up and opened it. When in walked a slender, young black wolf, who immediately went straight across the floor to an inner room, from which in a few moments came forth a dark, slender, handsome youth, who took his place at the table and looked hard at Connor with his glittering eyes.

"You are welcome," he said. "We have waited for you."

Before Connor could answer another knock was heard, and in came a second wolf, who passed on to the inner room like the first, and soon after, another dark, handsome youth came out and sat down to supper with them, glaring at Connor with his keen eyes, but said no word.

"These are my sons," said the old man, "tell them what you want, and what brought you here amongst us, for we live alone and don't care to have spies and strangers coming to our place."

Then Connor told his story, how he had lost his two fine cows, and had searched all day and found no trace of them; and he knew nothing of the place he was in, nor of the kindly gentleman who asked him to supper; but if they just told him where to find his cows he would thank them, and make the best of his way home at once.

Then they all laughed and looked at each other, and the old hag looked more frightful than ever when she showed her long, sharp teeth.

On this, Connor grew angry, for he was hot tempered; and he grasped his blackthorn stick firmly in his hand and stood up, and bade them open the door for him; for he would go his way, since they would give no heed and only mocked him.

Then the eldest of the young men stood up. "Wait," he said, "we are fierce and evil, but we never forget a kindness. Do you remember, one day down in the glen you found a poor little wolf in great agony and like to die, because a sharp thorn had pierced his side? And you gently extracted the thorn and gave him a drink, and went your way leaving him in peace and rest?"

"Aye, well do I remember it," said Connor, "and how the poor little beast licked my hand in gratitude."

"Well," said the young man, "I am that wolf, and I shall help you if I can, but stay with us tonight and have no fear."

So they sat down again to supper and feasted merrily, and then all fell fast asleep, and Connor knew nothing more till he awoke in the morning and found himself by a large hayrick in his own field.

"Now surely," thought he, "the adventure of last night was not all a dream, and I shall certainly find my cows when I go home; for that excellent, good young wolf promised his help, and I feel certain he would not deceive me."

But when he arrived home and looked over the yard and the stable and the field, there was no sign nor sight of the cows. So he grew very sad and dispirited. But just then he espied in the field close by three of the most beautiful strange cows he had ever set eyes on. "These must have strayed in," he said, "from some neighbour's ground"; and he took his big stick to drive them out of the gate off the field. But when he reached the gate, there stood a young black wolf watching; and when the cows tried to pass out at the gate he bit at them, and drove them back. Then Connor knew that his friend the wolf had kept his word. So he let the cows quietly back to the field; and there they remained, and grew to be the finest in the whole country, and their descendants are flourishing to this day, and Connor grew rich and prospered; for a kind deed is never lost, but brings good luck to the doer for evermore, as the old proverb says: "Blessings are won by a good deed done."

But never again did Connor find that desolate heath or that lone shieling, though he sought far and wide, to return his thanks, as was due to the friendly wolves; nor did he ever again meet any of the family, though he mourned much whenever a slaughtered wolf was brought into the town for the sake of the reward, fearing his excellent friend might be the victim. At that time the wolves in Ireland had increased to such an extent, owing to the desolation of the country by constant wars, that a reward was offered and a high price paid for every wolf's skin brought into the court of the justiciary; and this was in the time of Queen Elizabeth, when the English troops made ceaseless war against the Irish people, and there were more wolves in Ireland than men; and the dead lay unburied in hundreds on the highways, for there were no hands left to dig them graves.

THE LONG SPOON

Patrick Kennedy

~

$\mathcal{T}$he devil and the hearth-money collector for Bantry set out one summer morning to decide a bet they made the night before over a jug of punch. They wanted to see which would have the best load at sunset, and neither was to pick up anything that wasn't offered with the good-will of the giver. They passed by a house, and they heard the poor *ban-a-t'yee* cry out to her lazy daughter, "Oh, musha, the devil take you for a lazy *sthronsuch* of a girl! do you intend to get up to-day?"

"Oh, oh," says the taxman, "there is a job for you, Nick."

"*Ovock!*" says the other, "it wasn't from her heart that she said it; we must pass on."

The next cabin they were passing, the woman was on the bawnditch crying out to her husband, that was mending one of his brogues inside: "Oh, tattheration to you, Nick! you never rung them pigs, and there they are in the potato drills rootin' away; the devil run to Lusk with them."

"Another windfall for you," says the man of the inkhorn, but the old thief only shook his horns and wagged his tail. So they went on, and ever so many

prizes were offered to the black fellow without him taking one. Here it was a gorsoon playing *marvels* when he should be using his clappers in the corn-field; and there it was a lazy drone of a servant asleep with his face to the sod when he ought to be weeding. No one thought of offering the hearth-money man even a drink of buttermilk, and at last the sun was within half a foot of the edge of Cooliagh. They were just then passing Monamolin, and a poor woman that was straining her supper in a skeeoge outside her cabin-door, seeing the two standing at the bawn gate, bawled out, "Oh, here's the hearth-money man, the devil run away wid 'im."

"Got a bite at last," says Nick.

"Oh, no, no! it wasn't from her heart," says the collector.

"Indeed, an' it was from the very foundation-stones it came. No help for misfortunes; in with you," says he, opening the mouth of his big black bag; and whether the devil was ever after seen taking the same walk or not, nobody ever laid eyes on his fellow-traveller again.

THE STORY OF DEIRDRE

Joseph Jacobs

~

There was man in Ireland once who was called Malcolm Harper. The man was a right good man, and he had a goodly share of this world's goods. He had a wife, but no family. What did Malcolm hear but that a soothsayer had come home to the place, and as the man was a right good man, he wished that the soothsayer might come near them. Whether it was that he was invited or that he came of himself, the soothsayer came to the house of Malcolm.

"Are you doing any soothsaying?" says Malcolm.

"Yes, I am doing a little. Are you in need of soothsaying?"

"Well, I do not mind taking soothsaying from you, if you have soothsaying for me, and you would be willing to do it."

"Well, I will do soothsaying for you. What kind of soothsaying do you want?"

"Well, the soothsaying I wanted was that you would tell me my lot or what will happen to me, if you can give me knowledge of it."

"Well, I am going out, and when I return, I will tell you."

And the soothsayer went forth out of the house and he was not long outside when he returned. "Well," said the soothsayer, "I saw in my second sight that on account of a daughter of yours the greatest amount of blood shall be shed that has ever been shed in Erin since time and race began. And the three most famous heroes that ever were found will lose their heads on her account."

After a time a daughter was born to Malcolm, and because of the soothsaying he did not allow a living being to come to his house, only himself and the nurse. He asked this woman: "Will you yourself bring up the child to keep her in hiding far away, where eye will not see a sight of her nor ear hear a word about her?"

The woman said she would, so Malcolm got three men, and he took them away to a large mountain, distant and far from reach, without the knowledge or notice of anyone. He caused there a hillock, round and green, to be dug out of the middle, and the hole thus made to be covered carefully over so that a little company could dwell there together. This was done.

Deirdre and her foster-mother dwelt in the bothy mid the hills, without the knowledge or the suspicion of any living person about them and without anything occurring, until Deirdre was sixteen years of age. Deirdre grew like the white sapling, straight and trim as the rash on the moss. She was the creature of fairest form, of loveliest aspect, and of gentlest nature that existed between earth and heaven in all Ireland; and whatever colour of hue she had before, there was nobody that looked into her face but she would blush fiery red over it.

The woman who had charge of her gave Deirdre every information and skill of which she herself had knowledge and skill. There was not a blade of grass growing from root, nor a bird singing in the wood, nor a star shining from heaven but Deirdre had a name for it. Yet one thing the woman did not wish her to have either part or parley with—any single living man of the rest of the world.

But on a gloomy winter night, with black, scowling clouds, a hunter of game was wearily travelling the hills, and what happened but that he missed the trail of the hunt, and lost his course and companions. A drowsiness came upon the man as he wearily wandered over the hills, faint from hunger and wandering, and benumbed with cold. When he at last lay down beside the green hill in which Deirdre lived, a deep sleep fell upon him and a troubled dream came to him. He thought that he enjoyed the warmth of a fairy broch, the fairies being inside playing music. The hunter shouted out in his dream, if there was anyone in the broch, to let him in for the Holy One's sake.

Deirdre heard the voice and said to her foster-mother: "O foster-mother, what cry is that?"

"It is nothing at all, Deirdre, merely the birds of the air astray and seeking each other. But let them go past to the bosky glade. There is no shelter or house for them here."

"Oh, foster-mother, the bird asked to get inside for the sake of God of the Elements, and you yourself tell me that anything that is asked in his name we ought to do. If you will not allow the bird that is being benumbed with cold, and done to death with hunger, to be let in, I do not think much of your language or your faith. But since I give credence to your language and to your faith, which you taught me, I will myself let in the bird."

Deirdre arose and drew the bolt from the leaf of the door, and she let in the hunter. She placed a seat in the place for sitting, food in the place for eating, and drink in the place for drinking for the man who came to the house.

"Oh, for this life and raiment, you man that came in, keep restraint on your tongue!" said the old woman. "It is not a great thing for you to keep your mouth shut and your tongue quiet when you get a home and shelter of a hearth on a gloomy winter's night."

"Well," said the hunter, "I may do that—keep my mouth shut and my tongue quiet—since I came to the house and received hospitality from you. But by the hand of thy father and grandfather, and by your own two hands, if some other of the people of the world saw this beauteous creature you have here hid away, they would not long leave her with you, I swear."

"What men are these you refer to?" said Deirdre.

"Well, I will tell you, young woman," said the hunter. "They are Naois, son of Uisnech, and Allen and Arden his two brothers."

"What like are these men when seen, if we were to see them?" said Deirdre.

"Why, the aspect and form of the men when seen are these," said the hunter. "They have the colour of the raven on their hair, their skin like swan on the wave in whiteness, and their cheeks as the blood of the brindled red calf, and their speed and their leap are those of the salmon of the torrent and the deer of the grey mountainside. And Naois is head and shoulder above the rest of the people of Erin."

"However they are," said the nurse, "be off from here and take another road. And, King of Light and Sun, in good sooth and certainty, little are my thanks for yourself or for her that let you in!"

The hunter went away, and went straight to the palace of King Connachar. He sent word in to the King that he wished to speak to him if he pleased. The King answered the message and came out to speak to the man. "What is the reason of your journey?" said the King to the hunter.

"I have only to tell you, O King," said the hunter, "that I saw the fairest creature that ever was born in Erin, and I came to tell you of it."

"Who is this beauty and where is she to be seen, when she was not seen before till you saw her, if you did see her?"

"Well, I did see her," said the hunter, "but, if I did, no man else can see her unless he gets directions from me as to where she is dwelling."

"And will you direct me to where she dwells? And the reward of your directing me will be as good as the reward of your message," said the King.

"Well, I will direct you, O King, although it is likely that this will not be what they want," said the hunter.

Connachar, King of Ulster, sent for his nearest kinsmen, and he told them of his intent. Though early rose the song of the birds mid the rocky caves and the music of the birds in the grove, earlier than that did Connachar, King of Ulster, arise, with his little troop of dear friends, in the delightful twilight of the fresh and gentle May. The dew was heavy on each bush and flower and stem, as they went to bring Deirdre forth from the green knoll where she stayed. Many a youth was there who had a lithe, leaping, and lissom step when they started, whose step was faint, failing, and faltering when they reached the bothy on account of the length of the way and roughness of the road.

"Yonder now, down in the bottom of the glen, is the bothy where the woman dwells, but I will not go nearer than this to the old woman," said the hunter.

Connachar with his band of kinsfolk went down to the green knoll where

Deirdre dwelt, and he knocked at the door of the bothy. The nurse replied: "No less than a King's command and a King's army could put me out of my bothy tonight. And I should be obliged to you, were you to tell who it is that wants me to open my bothy door."

"It is I, Connachar, King of Ulster."

When the poor woman heard who was at the door, she rose with haste and let in the King and all that could get in of his retinue.

When the King saw that the woman was before him that he had been in quest of, he thought he never saw in the course of the day nor in the dream of night a creature so fair as Deirdre, and he gave his full heart's weight of love to her. Deirdre was raised on the topmost of the heroes' shoulders and she and her foster-mother were brought to the Court of King Connachar of Ulster.

With the love that Connachar had for her, he wanted to marry Deirdre right off there and then, will she nill she marry him. But she said to him: "I will be obliged to you if you will give me the respite of a year and a day."

He said: "I will grant you that, hard though it is, if you will give me your unfailing promise that you will marry me at the year's end." And she gave the promise.

Connachar got for her a woman-teacher and merry modest maidens fair that would lie down and rise with her, that would play and speak with her. Deirdre was clever in maidenly duties and wifely understanding, and Connachar thought he never saw with bodily eye a creature that pleased him more.

Deirdre and her women companions were one day out on the hillock behind the house, enjoying the scene, and drinking in the sun's heat. What did they see coming but three men a-journeying? Deirdre was looking at the men that were coming, and wondering at them. When the men neared them, Deirdre remembered the language of the huntsman, and she said to herself that these were the three sons of Uisnech, and she said that this was Naois, he having what was above the bend of the two shoulders above the men of Erin all.

The three brothers went past without taking any notice of them, without even glancing at the young girls on the hillock. What happened but that love for Naois struck the heart of Deirdre, so that she could not but follow after him. She girded up her raiment and went after the men that went past the base of the knoll, leaving her women attendants there.

Allen and Arden had heard of the woman that Connachar, King of Ulster, had with him, and they thought that if Naois, their brother, saw her, he would have her himself, more especially as she was not married to the King. They perceived the woman coming, and called on one another to hasten their step, as they had a long distance to travel, and the dusk of night was coming on. They did so.

She cried: "Naois, son of Uisnech, will you leave me?"

"What piercing, shrill cry is that—the most melodious my ear ever heard, and the shrillest that ever struck my heart of all the cries I ever heard?"

"Is it anything else but the wail of the wave-swans of Connachar?" said his brothers.

"No! Yonder is a woman's cry of distress," said Naois, and he swore he would not go farther until he saw from whom the cry came, and Naois turned back.

Naois and Deirdre met, and Deirdre kissed Naois three times, and a kiss each to his brothers. With the confusion that she was in, Deirdre went into a crimson blaze of fire, and her colour came and went as rapidly as the movement of the aspen by the stream side. Naois thought he never saw a fairer creature, and Naois gave Deirdre the love that he never gave to thing, to vision, or to creature but to herself. Then Naois placed Deirdre on the topmost height of his shoulder, and told his brothers to keep up their pace, and they kept up their pace.

Naois thought that it would not be well for him to remain in Erin on account of the way in which Connachar, King of Ulster, his kinsman, would go against him because of Deirdre, though he had not married her; and he turned back to Alba—that is, Scotland. He reached the side of Loch Ness and made his habitation there. He could kill the salmon of the torrent from out his own door, and the deer of the grey gorge from out his window. Naois and

Deirdre and Allen and Arden dwelt in a tower, and they were happy so long a time as they were there.

By this time the end of the period came when Deirdre had to marry Connachar, King of Ulster. Connachar made up his mind to take Deirdre away by the sword whether she was married to Naois or not. So he prepared a great and gleeful feast. Connachar thought to himself that Naois would not come, though he should bid him; and the scheme that arose in his mind was to send for his father's brother, Ferchar Mac Ro, and to send him on an embassy to Naois.

He did so, and Connachar said to Ferchar: "Tell Naois, son of Uisnech, that I am setting forth a great and gleeful feast to my friends and kinspeople throughout the wide extent of Erin all, and that I shall not have rest by day or sleep by night if he and Allen and Arden be not partakers of the feast."

Ferchar Mac Ro and his three sons went on their journey, and reached the tower where Naois was dwelling by the side of Loch Ness. The sons of Uisnech gave a cordial and kindly welcome to Ferchar Mac Ro and his three sons, and asked of him the news of Erin.

"The best news that I have for you," said the hardy hero, "is that Connachar, King of Ulster, is setting forth a sumptuous feast to his friends and kinspeople throughout the wide extent of Erin all, and he has vowed by the earth beneath him, by the high heaven above him, and by the sun that wends to the west, that he will have no rest by day nor sleep by night if the sons of Uisnech, the sons of his own father's brother, will not come back to the land of their home and the soil of their nativity, and to the feast likewise, and he has sent us on embassy to invite you."

"We will go with you," said Naois.

"We will," said his brothers.

But Deirdre did not wish to go with Ferchar Mac Ro, and she tried every prayer to turn Naois from going with him. She said: "I saw a vision, Naois, and do you interpret it to me." Then she sang:

"O Naois, son of Uisnech, hear
What was shown in a dream to me.

There came three white doves out of the south,

Flying over the sea,

And drops of honey were in their mouth

From the hive of the honey-bee.

O Naois, son of Uisnech, hear

What was shown in a dream to me.

I saw three grey hawks out of the south

Come flying over the sea, and the red red drops

   they bare in their mouth

They were dearer than life to me."

Said Naois:

"It is naught but the fear of a woman's heart,

And a dream of the night, Deirdre."

"The day that Connachar sent the invitation to his feast will be unlucky for us if we don't go, O Deirdre," said Naois.

"You will go there," said Ferchar Mac Ro. "And if Connachar shows kindness to you, show ye kindness to him; and if he will display wrath towards you, display ye wrath towards him, and I and my three sons will be with you."

"We will," said Daring Drop.

"We will," said Hardy Holly.

"We will," said Fiallan the Fair.

"I have three sons, and they are three heroes, and in any harm or danger that may befall you, they will be with you, and I myself will be along with them." And Ferchar Mac Ro gave his vow and his word in presence of his arms that, if any harm or danger came in the way of the sons of Uisnech, he and his three sons would not leave head on live body in Erin, despite sword or helmet, spear or shield, blade or mail, be they ever so good.

Deirdre was unwilling to leave Alba, but she went with Naois. Deirdre wept tears in showers and she sang:

"Dear is the land, the land over there,
Alba full of woods and lakes;
Bitter to my heart is leaving thee,
But I go away with Naois."

Ferchar Mac Ro did not stop till he got the sons of Uisnech away with him, despite the suspicion of Deirdre.

The coracle was put to sea,
The sail was hoisted to it;
And the second morrow they arrived
On the white shores of Erin.

As soon as the sons of Uisnech landed in Erin, Ferchar Mac Ro sent word to Connachar, King of Ulster, that the men whom he wanted were come, and let him now show kindness to them.

"Well," said Connachar, "I did not expect that the sons of Uisnech would come, though I sent for them, and I am not quite ready to receive them. But there is a house down yonder where I keep strangers, and let them go down to it today, and my house will be ready for them tomorrow."

But he that was up in the palace felt it long that he was not getting word as to how matters were going on for those down in the house of the strangers.

"Go you, Gelban Grednach, son of Lochlin's King, go you down and bring me information as to whether her former hue and complexion are on Deirdre. If they be, I will take her out with the edge of blade and point of sword, and if not, let Naois, son of Uisnech, have her for himself," said Connachar.

Gelban, the cheering and charming son of Lochlin's King, went down to the place of the strangers, where the sons of Uisnech and Deirdre were staying. He looked in through the bicker-hole on the door-leaf. Now she that he gazed upon used to go into a crimson blaze of blushes when anyone looked at her. Naois looked at Deirdre and knew that someone was looking at her from the back of the door-leaf. He seized one of the dice on the table before him and fired it through the bicker-hole, and knocked the eye out of Gelban Gred-nach the Cheerful and Charming, right through the back of his head. Gelban returned back to the palace of King Connachar.

"You were cheerful, charming, going away, but you are cheerless, charmless, returning. What has happened to you, Gelban? But have you seen her, and are Deirdre's hue and complexion as before?" said Connachar.

"Well, I have seen Deirdre, and I saw her also truly, and while I was looking at her through the bicker-hole on the door, Naois, son of Uisnech, knocked out my eye with one of the dice in his hand. But of a truth and verity, although he put out even my eye, it were my desire still to remain looking at her with the other eye, were it not for the hurry you told me to be in," said Gelban.

Connachar ordered three hundred active heroes to go down to the abode of the strangers and to take Deirdre up with them and to kill the rest.

"The pursuit is coming," said Deirdre.

"Yes, but I will myself go out and stop the pursuit," said Naois.

"It is not you, but we that will go," said Daring Drop, and Hardy Holly, and Fiallan the Fair. "It is to us that our father entrusted your defence from harm and danger when he himself left for home."

And the gallant youths, full noble, full manly, full handsome, with beauteous brown locks, went forth girt with battle arms fit for fierce fight and clothed for fierce contest, with combat dress which was burnished bright, brilliant, bladed, blazing, on which were many pictures of beasts and birds and creeping things, lions and lithe-limbed tigers, brown eagle and harrying hawk and adder fierce; and the young heroes laid low three-thirds of the company.

Connachar came out in haste and cried with wrath: "Who is there on the floor of fight, slaughtering my men?"

"We, the three sons of Ferchar Mac Ro."

"Well," said the King, "I will give a free bridge to your grandfather, a free bridge to your father, and a free bridge each to you three brothers, if you come over to my side tonight."

"Well, Connachar, we will not accept that offer from you, nor thank you for

it. Greater by far do we prefer to go home to our father and tell the deeds of heroism we have done, than accept anything on these terms from you. Naois, son of Uisnech, and Allen and Arden are as nearly related to yourself as they are to us, though you are so keen to shed their blood, and you shed our blood also, Connachar."

And the noble, manly, handsome youths with beauteous brown locks returned inside. "We are now," said they, "going home to tell our father that you are now safe from the hands of the King."

And the youths, all fresh and tall and lithe and beautiful, went home to their father to tell that the sons of Uisnech were safe. This happened at the parting of the day and night in the morning twilight time.

And Naois said they must go away, leave that house, and return to Alba. So Naois and Deirdre, Allen and Arden, started to return to Alba.

But word came to the King that the company he was in pursuit of were gone. The King then sent for Duanan Gacha Druid, the best magician he had, and he spoke to him as follows: "Too much wealth have I expended on you, Duanan Gacha Druid, to give schooling and learning and magic mystery to you, if these people get away today without care, without consideration or regard for me, without chance of overtaking them, and without power to stop them."

"Well, I will stop them," said the magician, "until the company you send in pursuit return." And the magician placed a wood before them through which no man could go, but the sons of Uisnech marched through the wood without halt or hesitation, and Deirdre held on to Naois's hand.

"What is the good of that, they will not do yet," said Connachar. "They are off without bending of their feet or stopping of their step, without heed or respect to me, and I am without power to keep up to them or opportunity to turn them back this night."

"I will try another plan on them," said the Druid, and he placed before them a grey sea instead of a green plain. The three heroes stripped and tied their clothes behind their heads, and Naois placed Deirdre on the top of his shoulder.

They stretched their sides to the stream,
And sea and land were to them the same;
The rough grey ocean was the same
As meadow-land green and plain.

"Though that be good, O Duanan, it will not make the heroes return," said Connachar. "They are gone without regard for me, and without honour to me, and without power on my part to pursue them or force them to return this night."

"We shall try another method on them, since yon one did not stop them," said the Druid. And the Druid froze the grey-ridged sea into hardy rocky knobs, the sharpness of sword being on the one edge and the poison power of adders on the other.

Then Arden cried that he was getting tired, and nearly giving over. "Come you, Arden, and sit on my right shoulder," said Naois. Arden came and sat on Naois's shoulder. Arden was long in this posture when he died; but though he was dead Naois would not let him go.

Allen then cried out that he was getting faint and nigh-well giving up, and he gave forth the piercing sigh of death. But Naois heard his cry and asked Allen to lay hold of him and he would bring him to land.

Allen was not long when the weakness of death came on him and his hold failed. Naois looked around, and when he saw his two well-beloved brothers dead, he cared not whether he lived or died, and he gave forth the bitter sigh of death, and his heart burst.

"They are gone," said Duanan Gacha Druid to the King, "and I have done what you desired me. The sons of Uisnech are dead and they will trouble you no more; and you have your wife hale and whole to yourself."

"Blessings for that upon you and may the good results accrue to me, Duanan. I count it no loss what I spent in the schooling and teaching of you. Now dry up the flood, and let me see if I can behold Deirdre," said Connachar.

And Duanan Gacha Druid dried up the flood from the plain, and the three sons of Uisnech were lying together dead, without breath of life, side by side on the green meadow plain and Deirdre bending above showering down her tears.

Then Deirdre said this lament: "Fair one, loved one, flower of beauty, beloved upright and strong, beloved noble and modest warrior. Fair one, blue-eyed, beloved of thy wife, lovely to me at the trysting-place came thy clear voice through the woods of Ireland. I cannot eat or smile henceforth. Break not today, my heart. Soon enough shall I lie within my grave. Strong are the waves of sorrow, but stronger is sorrow's self, Connachar."

The people then gathered round the heroes' bodies and asked Connachar what was to be done with the bodies. The order that he gave was that they should dig a pit and put the three brothers in it side by side.

Deirdre kept sitting on the brink of the grave, constantly asking the grave-diggers to dig the pit wide and free. When the bodies of the brothers were put in the grave, Deirdre said:

> "Come over hither, Naois, my love,
> Let Arden close to Allen lie;
> If the dead had any sense to feel,
> Ye would have made a place for Deirdre."

The men did as she told them. She jumped into the grave and lay down by Naois, and she was dead by his side.

The King ordered the body to be raised from out the grave and to be buried on the other side of the loch. It was done as the King bade, and the pit closed. Thereupon a fir shoot grew out of the grave of Deirdre and a fir shoot from the grave of Naois, and the two shoots united in a knot above the loch. The King ordered the shoots to be cut down, and this was done twice, until, at the third time, the wife whom the King had married caused him to stop this work of evil and his vengeance on the remains of the dead.

KNOCK MULRUANA

Douglas Hyde

～

*O*n the side of Glen Domhain, there is a little hill whose name is Mulroney's Hill, and this is the reason why it was given that name.

In old times there was a man living in a little house on the side of the hill, and Mulruana was his name. He was a pious holy man, and hated the world's vanities so much that he became a hermit, and he was always alone in that house, without anyone in his neighbourhood. He used to be always praying and subduing himself. He used to drink nothing but water, and used to eat nothing but berries and the wild roots which he used to get in the mountains and throughout the glens. His fame and reputation were going through the country for the holy earnest life that he was living.

However, great jealousy seized the Adversary at the piety of this man, and he sent many evil spirits to put temptations on him. But on account of all his prayers and piety it failed those evil spirits to get the victory over him, so that they all returned back to hell with the report of the steadfastness and loyalty of Mulruana in the service of God.

Then great anger seized Satan, so that he sent further demons, each more powerful than the other, to put temptation on Mulruana. Not one of them succeeded in even coming near the hut of the holy man. Nor did it fare any better with them whenever he came outside, for he used always to be attentive to his prayers and ever musing on holy things. Then every evil spirit of them used to go back to hell and used to tell the devil that there was no use contending with Mulruana, for that God himself and His angels were keeping him and giving him help.

That account made Satan mad entirely, so that he determined at last to go himself, hoping to destroy Mulruana, and to draw him out of the proper path. Accordingly he came one evening at nightfall, in the guise of a young woman, and asked the good man for lodging. Mulruana rudely refused the pretended woman, and banished her away from his door, although he felt a compassion for her because the night was wet and stormy, and he thought that the girl was without house and shelter from the rain and cold. But what the woman did was to go round to the back of the house and play music, and it was the sweetest and most melancholy music that man ever heard.

Because Mulruana had had a pity for the poor girl at the first, he listened now to her music, and took great delight in it, and had much joy of it, but he did not allow her into his hut. At the hour of midnight the devil went back to hell, but he had a shrewd notion that he had won the game and that he had caught the holy man. Mulruana had quiet during the remainder of the night, but instead of continuing at his prayers, as was his custom, he spent the end of the night, almost till the dawn of day, thinking of the beauty of the girl and of the sweetness of her music.

The day after that the devil came at the fall of night in the same likeness, and again asked lodging of Mulruana. Mulruana refused that, although he did not like to do it, but he remembered the vow he had made never to let a woman or a girl into his hut. The pretended woman went round to the back of the house, and she was playing music that was like fairy music until it was twelve o'clock, when she had to go away with herself to hell. The man inside was listening to the playing and taking great delight in it, and when she ceased there came over him melancholy and trouble of mind. He never slept a wink that night, and he never said a word of his prayers either, but eagerly thinking of the young woman, and his heart going astray with the beauty of her form and the sweetness of her voice.

On the morning of the next day Mulruana rose from his bed, and it is likely that it was the whisper of an angel he heard, because he remembered that it was not right for him to pay such heed to a girl and to forget his prayers. He bowed his knees and began to pray strongly and earnestly, and made a firm resolve that he would not think more about the girl, and that he would not listen to her music. But, after all, he did not succeed in obtaining a complete victory over his thoughts concerning the young woman, and consequently he was between two notions until the evening came.

When the night was well dark the Adversary came again in the shape of the girl, and she even more beautiful and more lovely than she was before, and asked the man for a night's lodging. He remembered his vow and the resolve he had made that day in the morning, and he refused her, and threatened her that she should not come again to trouble him, and he drove her away with rough sharp words, and with a stern, churlish countenance, as though there were a great anger on him. He went into his hut and the girl remained near the hut outside, and she weeping and lamenting and shedding tears.

When Mulruana saw the girl weeping and keening piteously he conceived a great pity for her, and compassion for her came to him, and desire, and he did not free his heart from those evil inclinations, since he had not made his prayers on that day with a heart as pure as had been his wont, and he listened willingly and gladly. It was not long until he came out, himself, in spite of his vow and his good resolutions, and invited the pretended woman to come into his hut. Small delay she made in going in!

It was then the King of Grace took pity at this man being lost without giving him time to amend himself, since he had ever been truly pious, diligent, humane, well disposed and of good works, until this great temptation came over him. For that reason God sent an angel to him with a message to ask him to repent. The angel came to Mulruana's house and went inside. Then the devil leapt to his feet, uttered a fearful screech, changed his colour, his shape, and his appearance. His own devilish form and demoniac appearance came upon him. He turned away from the angel like a person blinded with a great shining or blaze of light, and went out of the hut.

His senses nearly departed from Mulruana with the terror that overcame him. When he came to himself again the angel made clear to him how great was the sin to which he had given way, and how God had sent him to him to ask him to repent. But Mulruana never believed a word he said. He knew that it was the devil who had been in his company in the guise of a young woman. He remembered the sin to which he had consented, so that he considered himself to be so guilty that it would be impossible for him ever to obtain forgiveness from God. He thought that it was deceiving him the angel was, when he spoke of repentance and forgiveness. The angel was patient with him and spoke gently. He told him of the love and friendship of God and how He would never refuse forgiveness to the truly penitent, no matter how heavy his share of sins. Mulruana did not listen to him, but a drowning man's cry issued out of his mouth always, that he was lost, and he ever-cursing God, the devil and himself. The angel never ceased, but entreating and beseeching him to turn to God and make repentance—but it was no use for him. Mulruana was as hard and stubborn as he was before, all the time taking great oaths and blaspheming God.

All the time the angel was speaking he had the appearance of a burning candle in his hand. At long last, when the candle was burnt all but about an inch, a gloom fell over the countenance of the angel and he stood out from Mulruana, and threatened him, and told him that his term of grace was almost expired, and, said he, unless you make repentance before this inch of candle is burnt away, God will grant you no more respite, and you will be damned for ever.

Then there came silence on Mulruana for a while, as though he were about to follow the advice of the angel. But then on the spot he thought of the sin that he had done. On that, despair seized him, and the answer he gave the angel was, "As I have burned the candle I'll burn the inch." Then the angel spoke to him with a loud and terrible voice, announcing to him that he was now indeed accursed of God, and, said he, "thou shalt die to-morrow of thirst." Mulruana answered him with no submission, and said, "O lying angel, I know now that you are deceiving me. It is impossible that I should die of thirst in this place, and so much water round about me. There is, outside there, a well of spring water that was never dry, and there is a stream beside the gable of the house which would turn the wheel of a great mill no matter how dry the summer day, and down there is Loch Beithe on which a fleet of ships might float. It is a great folly for you to say that anybody could die of thirst in this place." But the angel departed from him without an answer.

Mulruana went to lie down after that, but, if he did, he never slept a wink through great trouble of spirit. Next morning, on his rising early, the sharpest thirst that man ever felt came upon him. He leapt out of his bed and went to the stoap [pail] for water, but there was not a drop in it. Out with him then to the well, but he did not find a drop there either. He turned on his foot towards the stream that was beside the house, but it was dry before him down to the gravel. The banks and the pebbles in the middle of it were as dry as though they had never seen a drop of water for a year. Mulruana remembered then the prophecy of the angel and he started. A quaking of terror came upon him, and his thirst was growing every moment. He went running at full speed to Loch Beithe, but when he came to the brink of the lake he uttered one awful cry and fell in a heap on the ground. Loch Beithe too was dry before him.

That is how a cowherd found him the next day, lying on the brink of the lake, his eyes starting out of his head, his tongue stretched out of his throat, and a lump of white froth round his mouth. His awful appearance was such that fear would not let the people go near him to bury him, and his body was left there until birds of prey and wild dogs took it away with them.

That is how it happened to Mulruana as a consequence of his sin, his impenitence, and his despair, and that is the reason why it is not right for any one to use the old saying, "As I've burnt the candle I'll burn the inch," and yonder is "Cnoc Mhaoilruanadha," Mulruana's Hill, as a witness to the truth of this story.

THE PRIEST'S SOUL

Lady Wilde

~

*I*n former days there were great schools in Ireland where every sort of learning was taught to the people, and even the poorest had more knowledge at that time than many a gentleman has now. But as to the priests, their learning was above all, so that the fame of Ireland went over the whole world, and many kings from foreign lands used to send their sons all the way to Ireland to be brought up in the Irish schools.

Now, at this time there was a little boy learning at one of them who was a wonder to everyone for his cleverness. His parents were only labouring people, and of course poor; but young as he was, and poor as he was, no king's or lord's son could come up to him in learning. Even the masters were put to shame; for when they were trying to teach him he would tell them something they never heard of before, and show them their ignorance. One of his great triumphs was in argument; and he would go on till he proved to you that black was white, and then when you gave in, for no one could beat him in talk, he would turn round and show you that white was black, or maybe that there was no colour at all in the world. When he grew up his poor father and mother were so proud of him that they resolved to make him a priest, which they did at last, though they nearly starved themselves to get the money. Well, such another learned man was not in Ireland, and he was as great in argument as ever, so that no one could stand before him. Even the bishops tried to talk to him, but he showed them at once they knew nothing at all.

Now, there were no schoolmasters in those times, but it was the priests taught the people; and as this man was the cleverest in Ireland, all the foreign kings sent their sons to him, as long as he had house room to give them. So he grew very proud, and began to forget how low he had been, and worst of all, even to forget God, who had made him what he was. And the pride of arguing got hold of him, so that from one thing to another he went on to prove that there was no Purgatory, and then no Hell, and then no Heaven, and then no God; and at last that men had no souls, but were no more than a dog or a cow, and when they died there was an end of them. "Whoever saw a soul?" he would say. "If you can show me one, I will believe." No one could make any answer to this; and at last they all came to believe that as there was no other world, everyone might do what they liked in this; the priest setting the example, for he took a beautiful young girl to wife. But as no priest or bishop in the whole land could be got to marry them, he was obliged to read the service over for himself. It was a great scandal, yet no one dared to say a word, for all the king's sons were on his side, and would have slaughtered anyone who tried to prevent his wicked goings-on. Poor boys; they all believed in him, and thought every word he said was the truth. In this way his notions began to spread about, and the whole world was going to the bad, when one night an angel came down from Heaven, and told the priest he had but twenty-four hours to live. He began to tremble, and asked for a little more time.

But the angel was stiff, and told him that could not be.

"What do you want time for, you sinner?" he asked.

"Oh, sir, have pity on my poor soul!" urged the priest.

"Oh, no! You have a soul then," said the angel. "Pray, how did you find that out?"

"It has been fluttering in me ever since you appeared," answered the priest. "What a fool I was not to think of it before."

"A fool, indeed," said the angel. "What good was all your learning, when it could not tell you that you had a soul?"

"Ah, my lord," said the priest, "if I am to die, tell me how soon I may be in Heaven?"

"Never," replied the angel. "You denied there was a Heaven."

"Then, my lord, may I go to Purgatory?"

"You denied Purgatory also; you must go straight to Hell," said the angel.

"But, my lord, I denied Hell also," answered the priest, "so you can't send me there either."

The angel was a little puzzled.

"Well," said he, "I'll tell you what I can do for you. You may either live now on earth for a hundred years, enjoying every pleasure, and then be cast into Hell for ever; or you may die in twenty-four hours in the most horrible torments, and pass through Purgatory, there to remain till the Day of Judgment, if only you can find some one person that believes, and through his belief mercy will be vouchsafed to you, and your soul will be saved."

The priest did not take five minutes to make up his mind.

"I will have death in the twenty-four hours," he said, "so that my soul may be saved at last."

On this the angel gave him directions as to what he was to do, and left him.

Then immediately the priest entered the large room where all the scholars and the kings' sons were seated, and called out to them:

"Now tell me the truth, and let none fear to contradict me; tell me what is your belief—have men souls?"

"Master," they answered, "once we believed that men had souls; but thanks to your teaching, we believe so no longer. There is no Hell, and no Heaven, and no God. This is our belief, for it is thus you taught us."

Then the priest grew pale with fear and cried out: "Listen! I taught you a lie. There is a God, and man has an immortal soul. I believe now all I denied before."

But the shouts of laughter that rose up drowned the priest's voice, for they thought he was only trying them for argument.

"Prove it, master," they cried. "Prove it. Who has ever seen God? Who has ever seen the soul?"

And the room was stirred with their laughter.

The priest stood up to answer them, but no word could he utter. All his eloquence, all his powers of argument had gone from him; and he could do nothing but wring his hands and cry out, "There is a God! there is a God! Lord have mercy on my soul!"

And they all began to mock him and repeat his own words that he had taught them:

"Show him to us; show us your God." And he fled from them groaning with agony, for he saw that none believed; and how, then, could his soul be saved?

But he thought next of his wife. "She will believe," he said to himself; "women never give up God."

And he went to her; but she told him that she believed only what he had taught her, and that a good wife should believe in her husband first and before and above all things in Heaven or earth.

Then despair came on him, and he rushed from the house, and began to ask every one he met if they believed. But the same answer came from one and all: "We believe only what you have taught us," for his doctrine had spread far and wide through the country.

Then he grew half mad with fear, for the hours were passing. And he flung himself down on the ground in a lonesome spot, and wept and groaned in terror, for the time was coming fast when he must die.

Just then a little child came by. "God save you kindly," said the child to him.

The priest started up.

"Do you believe in God?" he asked.

"I have come from a far country to learn about Him," said the child. "Will your honour direct me to the best school that they have in these parts?"

"The best school and the best teacher is close by," said the priest, and he named himself.

"Oh, not to that man," answered the child, "for I am told he denies God, and Heaven, and Hell, and even that man has a soul, because he cannot see it; but I would soon put him down."

The priest looked at him earnestly. "How?" he inquired.

"Why," said the child, "I would ask him if he believed he had life to show me his life."

"But he could not do that, my child," said the priest. "Life cannot be seen; we have it, but it is invisible."

"Then if we have life, though we cannot see it, we may also have a soul, though it is invisible," answered the child.

When the priest heard him speak these words he fell down on his knees before him, weeping for joy, for now he knew his soul was safe; he had met one at last that believed. And he told the child his whole story—all his wickedness, and pride, and blasphemy against the great God; and how the angel had come to him, and told him of the only way in which he could be saved, through the faith and prayers of someone that believed.

"Now, then," he said to the child, "take this penknife and strike it into my breast, and go on stabbing the flesh until you see the paleness of death on my face. Then watch—for a living thing will soar up from my body as I die, and you will then know that my soul has ascended to the presence of God. And when you see this thing, make haste and run to my school, and call on all my scholars to come and see that the soul of their master has left the body, and that all he taught them was a lie, for that there is a God who punishes sin, and a Heaven and a Hell, and that man has an immortal soul destined for eternal happiness or misery."

"I will pray," said the child, "to have courage to do this work." And he kneeled down and prayed. Then he rose up and took the penknife and struck it into the priest's heart, and struck and struck again till all the flesh was lacerated; but still the priest lived, though the agony was horrible, for he could not die until the twenty-four hours had expired.

At last the agony seemed to cease, and the stillness of death settled on his face. Then the child, who was watching, saw a beautiful living creature, with

four snow-white wings, mount from the dead man's body into the air and go fluttering round his head.

So he ran to bring the scholars; and when they saw it, they all knew it was the soul of their master; and they watched with wonder and awe until it passed from sight into the clouds.

And this was the first butterfly that was ever seen in Ireland; and now all men know that the butterflies are the souls of the dead waiting for the moment when they may enter Purgatory, and so pass through torture to purification and peace.

But the schools of Ireland were quite deserted after that time, for people said, What is the use of going so far to learn, when the wisest man in all Ireland did not know if he had a soul till he was near losing it, and was only saved at last through the simple belief of a little child?

THE PEOPLE OF THE SEA

David Thomson

~

*T*hose Kanes are from this part of Mayo," said Michael the Ferry.

"They are," said Patrick Sean, "and it's here they were in the beginning and it is by them the seals came here."

He looked at me. He laid his ashplant across his knees and began to speak very fast.

He said: "Long ago and a long time ago it was; if I was there then I wouldn't be here now, or if I were, I'd have a new story or an old story, or maybe I wouldn't have any story at all. Even if I were to lose only the back teeth or the front teeth or the teeth farthest back in my head—there was three brothers of the Kanes. And there was a smith in Ireland and he had a cow named Glas Ghaibhne. She had as much milk as twenty cows, but there had to be a man watching her from morning to sunset because she was under a spell. Any man who would guard her from morning to sunset would be given a sword for his pay. But it took a good man to guard her, for every day that she was feeding she would travel sixty miles eating a good bite here and a good bite there, and going hither and over, and wherever she went he must never go before her, nor hold her, nor stand in her way, but follow her always, thirty mile outward and thirty mile homeward the day she walked least. She was the best cow that ever was in Ireland before or since. Well, there was a young fellow of the Kanes there and, 'I'll guard her,' says he. So he guarded the cow till night and the smith gave him a sword. His brother was as good a man as he, and he went the next day and guarded her till night, and the smith gave him a sword. 'I'm as good a man as ye,' says the youngest brother, but when he went to guard her he slipped his foot and in a moment the cow was gone.

" 'Now,' said the smith, 'I'll give you one year and a day to find the cow Glas Ghaibhne.'

"The three brothers set out in their ship and sailed over the sea till they came to a strand like the one below the house here, very far from home. There was a man on the strand and he building a fence to keep out the sea.

" 'Well,' says the youngest of the brothers Kane, 'that's a foolish work you're at.'

" 'It's not a bit more foolish than what you're at,' says the man. 'I am under a spell by the man that took the cow. The name of that man is Balor Beimeann, and he has one eye in the middle of his forehead. And if you want to get the cow you must eat seven years' butter with three sorrel leaves and seven years' meat. You must lie with three hundred dark-haired women and three hundred red-haired women and three hundred fair-haired women, and have children by them in nine months time.'

" 'That's a terrible number of children,' says Kane.

" 'Well,' says the man who was building the fence, 'those nine hundred women are the guardians of Balor Beimeann's daughter up there on the hill. He doesn't let anyone visit her, but if you can at all you must go to her, for no one will ever kill Balor except the son of his daughter, and 'tis only by Balor's death that I will ever be free.'

" 'Very well,' says Kane to him. 'I'll go to Balor's daughter, if I can. But never mind these other women,' says he.

" 'You will go first to Balor's daughter,' says the man. 'She will be pleased with you and like you. But you must treat all these other women the same way or they'll tell Balor that they saw you there. Don't worry,' says he. 'I'll give you a belt to wear and you'll be as good after the last woman as after the first. Bring all these children to me.'

"Kane stayed on this island for the nine months until each of the women had a child, and the daughter of Balor on the hill had a son. He brought the children to the man on the strand; found him there still making his fence. Very well, when he brought them to the strand, the son of Balor's daughter surpassed all the children in strength.

" 'Take him home with you,' says the man on the strand. 'When you go out with the children into the deep sea, throw the whole lot of them out but keep the daughter's son. His name will be Lui of the Long Arm and 'tis he will kill his grandfather Balor Beimeann.'

"When Kane took the children out into the deep sea, he opened his cloak and every one of them fell into the sea. And they turned into a school of seals. So that's how the seals came to be." Patrick Sean looked at Michael the Ferry.

"It is, of course," said Michael.

Patrick Sean looked at me and went on. "Kane took the son of Balor's daughter home, but he was not thriving. So didn't he take ship again, himself with the child, and brought him to the man on the strand. There he was still at work with the fence. 'This child is not thriving,' says Kane.

" 'Is that so?' says the man on the strand. 'Oh, I see that,' says he. 'Take him up to Balor, on the hill,' he says. 'The child will not thrive till his grandfather calls him by name.'

"So Kane went to Balor and asked him for work.

" 'What can you do?' says Balor.

" 'I am the best gardener in the world,' says Kane.

" 'I have a better gardener than you,' says Balor.

" 'You have not,' says Kane. 'What can your gardener do?'

" 'The tree that he plants on Monday morning has the finest ripe apples on Saturday night.'

" 'That's nothing,' says Kane to him. 'The tree that I plant in the morning, I'll pick apples from it in the evening; every one of them the finest and ripest that ever you saw.'

" 'What child is that with you?' says Balor.

" 'My own child. His mother is dead.'

" 'I don't like children near my castle,' says Balor, 'but if you are such a gardener as you say, then I will keep you for a time. But what wages would you be looking for?' says he.

" 'I want no wages,' says Kane, 'only the cow Glas Ghaibhne to be given to me when my time is up.'

" 'In a year and a day you'll get her,' says Balor.

"Balor spoke no word to the child until one day Kane stumbled on the step of the door, and he with an armful of apples. All the people went to gather them up, and the son of Balor's daughter surpassed every one of them in his swiftness, and Balor let a shout out of him then. 'Take away with you that little Long Arm,' he said.

" 'Oh, he has his name now,' said Kane, and after that the child began to thrive.

"When he had his time worked, Kane went to ask Balor for the cow.

" 'Certainly,' says Balor. 'But I must tell you,' says he, 'there is only one way I can give her to you, for it is my daughter has her halter, and whatever man she chooses to throw the halter to, it is only he that can have the cow.'

"So Kane and Balor stood below the daughter's window, and she saw it was Kane that was there. She threw the halter to Kane.

"Balor let a shout out of him again. 'How could you do that, my daughter?' says he.

" 'Oh, Father,' says she, 'there's a crooked cast in every woman's hand. I did intend to throw it to you.'

"Very well. Kane got the cow and he brought her and the child back to Ireland to the smith.

"When Balor Beimeann heard that the child that was in Ireland was his own daughter's child, over he came to destroy all Ireland. He had an eye in the middle of his forehead which he kept covered always with nine shields of thick leather so that he might not open his eye and turn it on anything, for no matter what Balor looked on he burned it to ashes. When he came to Ireland, all that he saw was the tops of the wild iris and the tops of the rushes, and these are burned red ever since, but before he could see more, Lui of the Long Arm, his daughter's son, put a spear into his eye and killed him.

"Balor said then, 'Let me rest my head on your body and I shall leave you a virtue.' But Lui suspected him. He got a big stone and put Balor's head on that. A tear fell from Balor Beimeann's eye onto the stone and it split the stone in two. That is my story," said Patrick Sean Cregan, and his voice gathered speed to end as he had begun in a gabbled monotone, "God to my lips! Death will come. Great the tidings! The blessing of God on the souls of the dead!"

THE CHILD'S DREAM

Lady Wilde

~

The island of Innis-Sark (Shark Island) was a holy and peaceful place in old times; and so quiet that the pigeons used to come and build in a great cave by the sea, and no one disturbed them. And the holy saints of God had a monastery there, to which many people resorted from the mainland, for the prayers of the monks were powerful against sickness or evil, or the malice of an enemy.

Amongst others, there came a great and noble prince out of Munster, with his wife and children and their nurse; and they were so pleased with the island that they remained a year or more; for the prince loved fishing, and often brought his wife along with him.

One day, while they were both away, the eldest child, a beautiful boy of ten years old, begged his nurse to let him go and see the pigeons' cave, but she refused.

"Your father would be angry," she cried, "if you went without leave. Wait till he comes home, and see if he will allow you."

So when the prince returned, the boy told him how he longed to see the cave, and the father promised to bring him next day.

The morning was beautiful and the wind fair when they set off. But the child soon fell asleep in the boat, and never wakened all the time his father was fishing. The sleep, however, was troubled, and many a time he started and cried aloud. So the prince thought it better to turn the boat and land, and then the boy awoke.

After dinner the father called for the child. "Tell me now," he said, "why was your sleep troubled, so that you cried out bitterly in your dream?"

"I dreamed," said the boy, "that I stood upon a high rock, and at the bottom flowed the sea, but the waves made no noise; and as I looked down I saw fields and trees and beautiful flowers and bright birds in the branches, and I longed to go down and pluck the flowers. Then I heard a voice, saying, 'Blessed are the souls that come here, for this is Heaven.'

"And in an instant I thought I was in the midst of the meadows amongst the birds and the flowers; and a lovely lady, bright as an angel, came up to me and said, 'What brings you here, dear child; for none but the dead come here?'

"Then she left me, and I wept for her going; when suddenly all the sky grew black, and a great troop of wild wolves came round me, howling and opening their mouths wide as if to devour me. And I screamed, and tried to run, but I could not move, and the wolves came closer, and I fell down like one dead with fright, when, just then, the beautiful lady came again, and took my hand and kissed me.

" 'Fear not,' she said, 'take these flowers, they come from heaven. And I will bring you to the meadow where they grow.'

"And she lifted me up into the air, but I know nothing more; for then the boat stopped and you lifted me on shore, but my beautiful flowers must have fallen from my hands, for I never saw them more. And this is all my dream; but I would like to have my flowers again, for the lady told me they had the secret that would bring me to heaven."

The prince thought no more of the child's dream, but went off to fish next day as usual, leaving the boy in the care of his nurse. And again the child begged and prayed her so earnestly to bring him to the pigeons' cave, that at last she consented; but told him he must not go a step by himself, and she would bring two of the boys of the island to take care of him.

So they set off, the child and his little sister with the nurse. And the boy gathered wild flowers for his sister, and ran down to the edge of the cave where the cormorants were swimming; but there was no danger, for the two young islanders were minding him.

So the nurse was content, and being weary she fell asleep. And the little sister lay down beside her, and fell asleep likewise.

Then the boy called to his companions, the two young islanders, and told them he must catch the cormorants. So away they ran, down the path to the sea, hand in hand, and laughing as they went. Just then a piece of rock loosened and fell beside them, and trying to avoid it they slipped over the edge of the narrow path down a steep place, where there was nothing to hold on by except a large bush, in the middle of the way. They got hold of this, and thought they were now quite safe, but the bush was not strong enough to bear their weight, and it was torn up by the roots. And all three fell straight down into the sea and were drowned.

Now, at the sound of the great cry that came up from the waves, the nurse awoke, but saw no one. Then she woke up the little sister. "It is late," she cried, "they must have gone home. We have slept too long, it is already evening; let us hasten and overtake them, before the prince is back from the fishing."

But when they reached home the prince stood in the doorway. And he was very pale, and weeping.

"Where is my brother?" cried the little girl.

"You will never see your brother more," answered the prince. And from that day he never went fishing any more, but grew silent and thoughtful, and was never seen to smile. And in a short time he and his family quitted the island, never to return.

But the nurse remained. And some say she became a saint, for she was always seen praying and weeping by the entrance to the great sea cave. And one day, when they came to look for her, she lay dead on the rocks. And in her hand she held some beautiful strange flowers freshly gathered, with the dew on them. And no one knew how the flowers came into her dead hand. Only some fishermen told the story of how the night before they had seen a bright fairy child seated on the rocks singing; and he had a red sash tied round his waist, and a golden circlet binding his long yellow hair. And they all knew that he was the prince's son, who had been drowned in that spot just a twelve-month before. And the people believe that he had brought the flowers from the spirit-land to the woman, and given them to her as a death sign, and a blessed token from God that her soul would be taken to heaven.

THE FATE OF
THE CHILDREN OF LIR

Joseph Jacobs

~

It happened that a long time ago in the age of gods and heroes, the Sea God, Lir, married a foster daughter of Bodb the Red, King of the Gods. She bore him four children: a daughter called Fionula, then a son called Aed and two others, twin boys, called Fiachra and Conn. But at the birth of the twins she died and Lir was left sorrowing.

After some time Lir visited the court of his father-in-law and married the sister of his dead wife, whom he thought would be a good mother to his children. For a time all went well. The princess, called Aeife, treated her stepchildren kindly. But then Aeife began to be jealous of the tenderness and attention shown by Lir to Fionula and her brothers, and to fear he loved them better than he did her. At last the wish for their death came into her heart and she began to plot to destroy them.

First she tried to bribe servants to murder them, but this failed. Fearing to kill them herself, she led them away to a lonely lake, where she sent them into the water to bathe. Then from under her cloak she drew out a wand, such as the Druids used, and making an incantation over the children she turned them all into swans.

But although she had enough magical power to change their shapes, she could not take from them their speech or human hearts.

Fionula, the lovely girl who was now a swan, swam into the reeds just below the bank where Aeife was standing, and rearing her proud head she said: "Wicked and treacherous woman, give us back our human shapes, or Lir our father will punish you."

But Aeife smiled scornfully. "The lake is deep, and the children of Lir were drowned," she said. "That is the story I shall tell their father."

No words of beseeching would change the wicked Aeife's heart, or make her withdraw the spell.

Fionula spoke once more. "How long must we remain swans?" she asked bravely.

"Better if you had not asked me," replied Aeife. "But I will tell you. Three hundred years shall you remain upon this lake; and three hundred years upon the Sea of Moyle, the sea which lies between Erin and Alba; and three hundred years more beside the Isle of Glora in Erris."

"If you had killed us," cried Aed, "it had been kinder!"

"Nay," replied Aeife, "for after this moment you shall not remember your grief at being swans. But your human speech and human hearts, these shall you keep and you shall be able to sing more sweetly and more softly than swans have ever yet sung. Fare you well. I could have loved you had not your father loved you too dearly."

And with one wild gesture, half-triumphant, half-tragic, Aeife turned her back upon the lake and upon the four swans. But as she mounted the hill that lay between the lake and her palace she heard the swans singing, singing so sweetly and so softly that for a moment she paused to listen and then, plunging her fingers into her ears, she hurried on.

When Aeife got home she found Lir waiting for her. "You have been gone long," he said, "you and the children."

Aeife began to weep and wail of how the children had been disobedient and how they had drowned in the strong current and reeds in the lake.

But Lir in great grief cried out: "This is not true! You who pretended to love my children with a mother's love, you have led them away, you have led them away!" Here he was able to say no more, but rushed away from Aeife and ran towards the lake.

The lake lay shimmering like silver under beams of the summer moon. And as he stood there, four swans came sailing towards him, their wings widened as if to enfold him. And one, the one who had been his daughter, began to speak in the tones he loved so well. She told him all the tragic story, and Conn, the younger of the twins, broke in, begging his father to restore their human shape.

"I want to run and play with my brother," he said. "Just as we used to run and play before magic touched us."

Then Lir wrung his hands in agony. "Would that I had power enough," he said sorrowfully. "But I am, after all, such a puny god, I who thought I ruled the sea."

"Do not grieve, my lord," said Fionula very gently. "We are not so unhappy. We love you and remember you are our father. If you will come down every night at sunset, then we will talk to you; then we will sing to you, and you will forget."

But anger against the false woman Aeife arose again in the heart of the Sea God. He caressed the heads of the swans, and his tears fell fast as he turned to leave them, and even their song which followed him up the hillside could not soothe his rage.

He went to Bodb the Red, who asked for proof of the evil deed. Lir led him to the lake, where the swans floated in the red light of the dawn. And they told their own tale, without passion or anger, until the end came and the toll of their sentence—three hundred years upon the Lake of Darvra, three hundred years upon the Sea of Moyle, three hundred years beside the Isle of Glora.

Lir asked Bodb to use his magic to bring back his children. But Bodb the Red turned to him a face of pain and pity and said sadly that his magic was not enough to restore them to their father.

Yet Bodb the Red could punish Aeife. She came before the King quietly, as one in deep sorrow. She had put away her jewels, and over her golden hair she wore the veil of mourning.

The King began to tell her the story of the swans, while Aeife boldly pretended that the children had been claimed by the waters of the lake.

The King twirled his Druid's wand and said: "I shall not ask you, Aeife, what has become of the children of Lir. I shall not ask you what you can do to restore them to their sorrowing father. He stands there; you can look at him and see how stricken he is. You can listen, Aeife, for the soft voice of Fionula, and look long for the lithe form of young Aed to stride over the fairy hills. You can run fleet of foot across the green grass, but never again will Conn or Fiachra overtake you, or their gay young laughter gladden your heart. But my question is far away from talk of the lost children of Lir. Answer me truly, Aeife, what do you fear more than my wand?"

Aeife, in great terror at the wand waving above her head, was compelled to answer: "To be a demon, a demon of the air, with no rest for body or soul."

She shrieked wildly, and she tried to clutch the wand, but it swept over her like the sword of an avenger, and her human shape fell from her like a beautiful dress. Then she rose as if she had wings, the wings of a vampire or a great bat, and again she shrieked, like a shrill wind before a storm, and flew far away. Over the hills she went, and over the Lake of Darvra. The sky was black with clouds, and from the distant mountains came the heavy roll of thunder. No heart, no speech, no song had the King of the Gods left her—only her wickedness, and a demon's shape to carry her about for ever like a bird of ill omen.

All the Gods of the Gaels came to hear of the sweet singing of the swans and went down to the Lake of Darvra to listen to it. It became a custom amongst Gods and mortals to hold a yearly feast in honour of the swans.

But at the end of three hundred years the second part of the spell began. The swans had to leave the beautiful lake they knew so well, and fly away to the cold north to make their home upon the bleak and stormy Sea of Moyle.

Upon the Sea of Moyle, far away from Gods and men, the four swans suffered the worst of weather. In lonely exile they spent day and night buffeted by wind and storm, haunted by the cries of shipwrecked mariners and terrified by the monsters of the deep. Forbidden to land, their feathers in the bitter winters froze against the sharp rocks, and only their love of each other remained of the happy past.

During this sad time Fionula, the eldest of the four, became as a mother to the rest, wrapping her plumage round the youngest ones when the frost left a white rime on the rocks. With Conn on her right hand always, and Fiachra on her left, she kept Aed in front of her. "For," she said, "so I can shelter you all with my wings."

At last they entered on the third stage of their ordeal and went to the wild Isle of Glora; and there, too, they suffered loneliness and fear. The years rolled by. On the shores of Erris they first heard the sound of a church-bell, which filled them with wonder.

As the time of their sentence drew to an end, they wished to return to the palace of their father, Lir. Soon the air was filled with the sound of wings in strong flight, as the four swans winged their way towards Ireland. But when they came to look for their old home, all they could see was a few great mounds, clumps of nettles and windswept bushes. The palace was there, but from their eyes it was hidden, because they were destined for higher things than a return to the land of their youth.

With great sadness they flew slowly back to Erris, and then again they heard the thin sound of a bell. Terrified, the swans listened. The bell stopped and from a tiny chapel a man dressed in the robe of a hermit came out and made his way down towards them on the shore. The old hermit heard their story and the four swans made their home beside the little chapel and every day said over the simple prayers that he taught them. Their sorrow lightened; their beautiful song was heard again.

Now it happened that a princess of Munster was to wed a powerful chief, and begged from him as a bridal token the four wonderful swans that sung so well. The chief tried to bribe the hermit to part with the swans with gifts of bronze and silver for the chapel.

But the old man waved him away saying: "There is no price for a human soul. Under their plumage beat human hearts. Enchantment is still heavy upon them, but God is merciful, and their penance draws nigh to its end."

However, the chief seized hold of the silver chains which coupled the swans and dragged them away. But when the swans were ordered to sing before the bride, not a note could they utter. Then the face of the princess froze stiff in horror, for from the four swans fell away their snowy plumage and before her cowered an aged woman and three withered old men. Nine hundred years had passed over their heads and the days of gods and heroes had gone for ever. The bride ran shrieking from the palace. But the hermit, seeing that the Angel of Death would soon claim them, sprinkled each meek white head with the water of holiness, and to each gave promise of life everlasting.

Fionula stretched out her arms towards the other three, and asked that they be laid in one grave, with Conn placed on her right hand and Fiachra on her left, and Aed before her face where she could see him. So that with her wings she could shelter them, as she had done upon the stormy Sea of Moyle.

Thus did the hermit lay the four children of Lir to rest at last.

SEA STORIES

Lady Gregory

~

$\mathcal{I}$ was told by:

A Man on the Height near Dun Conor: It's said there's everything in the sea the same as on the land, and we know there's horses in it. This boy here saw a horse one time out in the sea, a grey one, swimming about. And there were three men from the north island caught a horse in their nets one night when they were fishing for mackerel, but they let it go; it would have broke the boat to bits if they had brought it in, and anyhow they thought it was best to leave it. One year at Kinvarra, the people were missing their oats that were eaten in the fields, and they watched one night and it was five or six of the sea-horses they saw eating the oats, but they could not take them, they made off to the sea.

And there was a man on the north island fishing on the rocks one time, and a mermaid came up before him, and was partly like a fish and the rest like a woman. But he called to her in the name of God to be off, and she went and left him.

Surely those things are on the sea as well as on the land. My father was out fishing one night off Tyrone and something came beside the boat, that had eyes shining like candles. And then a wave came in, and a storm rose of a moment, and whatever was in the wave, the weight of it had like to sink the boat. And then they saw that it was a woman in the sea that had the shining eyes. So my father went to the priest, and he bid him always to take a drop of holy water and a pinch of salt out in the boat with him, and nothing would harm him.

A Galway Bay Lobster-Seller: They are on the sea as well as on the land, and their boats are often to be seen on the bay, sailing boats and others. They look like our own, but when you come near them they are gone in an instant.

My mother one time thought she saw our own boat come into the pier with my father and two other men in it, and she got the supper ready, but when she went down to the pier and called after them there was nothing there. And the boat didn't come in till two hours after.

There were three or four men went out one day to fish, and it was dead calm; but all of a sudden they heard a blast and they looked, and within about three mile of the boat they saw twelve men from the waist, the rest of them was under water. And they had sticks in their hands and were striking one another. And where they were, and the blast, it was rough, but smooth and calm on each side.

There's a sort of light on the sea sometimes; some call it a "Jack O'Lantern" and some say it is sent by *them* to mislead them.

There were two brothers of my own went to fish for the herrings, and what they brought up was like the print of a cat, and it turned with the inside of the skin outside, and no hair. So they pulled up the nets, and fished no more that day. There was one of *them* lying on the strand here, and some of the men of the village came down of a sudden and surprised him. And when he saw he was taken he began a great crying. But they only lifted him down to the sea and put him back into it. Just like a man they said he was. And a little way out there was another just like him, and when he saw that they treated the one on

146

shore so kindly, he bowed his head as if to thank them. Whatever's on the land, there's the same in the sea, and between the islands of Aran they can often see the horses galloping about at the bottom.

There was a sort of big eel used to be in Tully churchyard, used to come up and root up the bodies, but I didn't hear of him of late—he may be done away with now.

There was one Curran told me one night he went down to the strand where he used to be watching for timber thrown up and the like. And on the strand, on the dry sands, he saw a boat, a grand one with sails spread and all, and it up farther than any tide had ever reached. And he saw a great many people round about it, and it was all lighted up with lights. And he got afraid and went away. And four hours after, after sunrise, he went there again to look at it, and there was no sign of it, or of any fire, or of any other thing. The Mara-warra (mermaid) was seen on the shore not long ago, combing out her hair. She had no fish's tail, but was like another woman.

John Corley: There is no luck if you meet a mermaid and you out at sea, but storms will come, or some ill will happen. There was a ship on the way to America, and a mermaid was seen following it, and the bad weather began to come. And the captain said, "It must be some man in the ship she's following, and if we knew which one it was, we'd put him out to her and save ourselves." So they drew lots, and the lot fell on one man, and then the captain was sorry for him, and said he'd give him a chance until tomorrow. And the next day she was following them still, and they drew lots again, and the lot fell on the same man. But the captain said he'd give him a third chance, but the third day the lot fell on him again. And when they were going to throw him out he said, "Let me alone for a while." And he went to the end of the ship and he began to sing a song in Irish, and when he sang, the mermaid began to be quiet and to rock like as if she was asleep. So he went on singing till they came to America, and just as they got to the land the ship was thrown up into the air, and came down on the water again. There's a man told me that was surely true.

John Nagle: For one there's on the land there's ten on the sea. When I lived at Ardfry there was never a night but there was a voice heard crying and roaring, by them that were out in the bay. A baker he was from Loughrea, used to give short weight and measure, and so he was put there for a punishment.

I saw a ship that was having a race with another go suddenly down into the sea, and no one could tell why. And afterwards one of the Government divers was sent down to look for her, and he told me he'd never as long as he'd live go down again, for there at the bottom he found her, and the captain and the saloon passengers, and all sitting at the table eating their dinner just as they did before.

At an Evening Gathering in Inishmaan, by a Son of the House: There was a man on this island was down on the beach one evening with his dog, and some black thing came up out of the sea, and the dog made for it and began to fight it. And the man began to run home and he called the dog, and it followed him, but every now and again it would stop and begin to fight again. And when he got to the house he called the dog in and shut the door, and whatever was outside began hitting against the door but it didn't get in. But the dog went in under the bed in the room, and before morning it was dead.

The Man of the House: A horse I've seen myself on the sea and on the rocks—a brown one, just like another. And I threw a stone at it, and it was gone in a minute. We often heard there was fighting amongst *these*. And one morning before daybreak I went down to the strand with some others, and the whole of the strand, and it low tide, was covered with blood.

A Man Near Loughmore: It's the people in the middle island know about these things. There were three boys from there lost in a curragh at the point near the lighthouse, and for long after their friends were tormented when they came there fishing, and they would see ships when the people of this island that were out at the same time couldn't see them. There were three or four out in a curragh near the lighthouse, and a conger-eel came and upset it, and they were all saved but one, but he was brought down and for the whole day

they could hear him crying and screeching under the sea. And they were not the only ones, but a fisherman that was there from Galway had to go away and leave it, because of the screeching.

There was a woman walking over by the north shore—God have mercy on her, she's dead since—and she looked out and saw an island in the sea, and she was a long time looking at it. It's known to be there, and to be enchanted, but only few can see it.

There was a man had his horse drawing seaweed up there on the rocks, the way you see them drawing it every day, in a basket on the mare's back. And on this day every time he put the load on, the mare would let its leg slip and it would come down again, and he was vexed and he had a stick in his hand and he gave the mare a heavy blow. And that night she had a foal that was dead, not come to its full growth, and it had spots over it, and every spot was of a different colour. And there was no sire on the island at that time, so whatever was the sire must have come up from the sea.

Mary Moran: There was a girl here that had been to America and came back, and one day she was coming over from Liscannor in a curragh, and she looked back and there beyond the curragh was the Gan ceann, the headless one. And he followed the boat a great way, but she said nothing. But a gold pin that was in her hair fell out, and into the sea, that she had brought from America, and then it disappeared. And her sister was always asking her where was the pin she brought from America, and she was afraid to say. But at last she told her, and her sister said, "It's well for you it fell out, for what was following you would never have left you, till you threw it a ring or something made of gold." It was the sister herself that told me this.

Up in the village beyond they think a great deal of these things and they won't part with a drop of milk on May Eve, and last Saturday week that was May Eve there was a poor woman dying up there, and she had no drop of milk of her own, and as is the custom, she went out to get a drop from one or other of the neighbours. But no one would give it because it was May Eve. I declare I cried when I heard it, for the poor woman died on the second day after.

And when my sister was going to America, she went on the first of May and we had a farewell party the night before, and in the night a little girl that was there saw a woman of that village go out, and she watched her, and saw her walk round a neighbour's house, and pick some straw from the roof.

And she told of it, and it happened that a child had died in that house and the father said the woman must have had a hand in it, and there was no good feeling to her for a long while. Her own husband is lying sick now, so I hear.

OISIN IN TIR NA NOG

P. W. Joyce

~

A short time after the fatal battle of Gavra, where so many of our heroes fell, we were hunting on a dewy morning near the brink of Loch Lein, where the trees and hedges around us were all fragrant with blossoms, and the little birds sang melodious music on the branches. We soon roused the deer from the thickets, and as they bounded over the plain, our hounds in full cry followed after them.

We were not long so engaged, when we saw a rider coming swiftly towards us from the west; and we soon perceived that it was a maiden on a white steed. We all ceased from the chase on seeing the lady, who reined in as she approached. And Finn and the Fena were greatly surprised, for they had never before seen so lovely a maiden. A slender golden diadem encircled her head. She wore a brown robe of silk, spangled with stars of red gold, which was fastened in front by a golden brooch, and fell from her shoulders till it swept the ground. Her yellow hair flowed far down over her robe in bright, golden ringlets. Her blue eyes were as clear as the drops of dew on the grass, and while her small, white hand held the bridle and curbed her steed with a golden bit, she sat more gracefully than a swan on Loch Lein.

The white steed was covered with a smooth, flowing mantle. He was shod with four shoes of pure yellow gold, and in all Erin a better or more beautiful steed could not be found.

As she came slowly to the presence of Finn, he addressed her courteously: "Who art thou, O lovely youthful princess? Tell us thy name and the name of thy country, and relate to us the cause of thy coming."

She answered in a sweet and gentle voice: "Noble King of the Fena, I have had a long journey this day, for my country lies far off in the Western Sea. I am the daughter of the King of Tir na nOg, and my name is Niamh of the Golden Hair."

"And what is it that has caused thee to come so far across the sea? Has thy husband forsaken thee? Or what other evil has befallen thee?"

"My husband has not forsaken me, for I have never been married or betrothed to any man. But I love thy noble son, Oisin, and this is what has brought me to Erin. It is not without reason that I have given him my love, and that I have undertaken this long journey. For I have often heard of his bravery, his gentleness, and the nobleness of his person. Many princes and high chiefs have sought me in marriage, but I was quite indifferent to all men and never consented to wed, till my heart was moved with love for thy gentle son, Oisin."

When I heard these words, and when I looked on the lovely maiden with her glossy, golden hair, I was all over in love with her. I came near, and, taking her small hand in mine, I told her she was a mild star of brightness and beauty, and that I preferred her to all the princesses in the world for my wife.

"Then," said she, "I place you under geasa, which true heroes never break through, to come with me on my white steed to Tir na nOg, the land of never-ending youth. It is the most delightful and most renowned country under the sun. There is abundance of gold and silver and jewels, of honey and wine; and the trees bear fruit and blossoms and green leaves together all the year round.

"You will get a hundred swords and a hundred robes of silk and satin, a hundred swift steeds, and a hundred slender, keen-scenting hounds. You will get herds of cows without number, flocks of sheep with fleeces of gold, a coat of mail that cannot be pierced, and a sword that never missed a stroke and from which no one ever escaped alive.

"There are feasting and harmless pastimes each day. A hundred warriors fully armed shall await you at call, and harpers shall delight you with their sweet music. You will wear the diadem of the King of Tir na nOg, which he never yet gave to anyone under the sun, and which will guard you day and night, in tumult and battle and danger of every kind.

"Lapse of time shall bring neither decay nor death, and you shall be for ever young, and gifted with unfading beauty and strength. All these delights you shall enjoy, and many others that I do not mention; and I myself will be your wife if you come with me to Tir na nOg."

I replied that she was my choice above all the maidens in the world, and that I would willingly go with her to the Land of Youth.

When my father, Finn, and the Fena heard me say this, and knew I was going from them, they raised three shouts of grief and lamentation. And Finn came up to me and took my hand in his, saying sadly: "Woe is me, my son, that you are going away from me, for I do not expect that you will ever return to me."

The manly beauty of his countenance became quite dimmed with sorrow, and though I promised to return after a little time, and fully believed that I should see him again, I could not check my tears as I gently kissed my father's cheek.

I then bade farewell to my dear companions, and mounted the white steed, while the lady kept her seat before me. She gave the signal, and the steed galloped swiftly and smoothly towards the west, till he reached the strand; and when his gold-shod hooves touched the waves, he shook himself and neighed three times. He made no delay, but plunged forward at once, moving over the face of the sea with the speed of a cloud-shadow on a March day. The wind overtook the waves and we overtook the wind, so that we straightway lost sight of land; and we saw nothing but billows tumbling before us and billows tumbling behind us.

Other shores came into view, and we saw many wonderful things on our journey—islands and cities, lime-white mansions, bright *grianáns* (summerhouses) and lofty palaces. A hornless fawn once crossed our course, bounding nimbly along from the crest of one wave to the crest of another, and close after in full chase a white hound with red ears. We saw also a lovely young maiden on a brown steed, with a golden apple in her hand; and as she passed swiftly by, a young warrior on a white steed plunged after her, wearing a long, flowing mantle of yellow silk and holding a gold-hilted sword in his hand.

I knew naught of these things, and, marvelling much, I asked the princess what they meant. "Heed not what you see here, Oisin," she said, "for all these wonders are as nothing compared with what you shall see in Tir na Nog."

At last we saw at a great distance, rising over the waves on the very verge of the sea, a palace more splendid than all the others; and, as we drew near, its front glittered like the morning sun. I asked the lady what royal house this was and who was the prince that rules it.

"This country is the Land of Virtues," she replied. "Its king is the giant, Fomor of the Blows, and its queen the daughter of the King of the Land of Life. This Fomor brought the lady away by force from her own country, and keeps her in his palace. But she has put him under geasa that he cannot break through, never to ask her to marry him till she can find a champion to fight him in single combat. Yet she still remains in bondage, for no hero has yet come hither who has the courage to meet the giant."

"A blessing on you, golden-haired Niamh," I replied. "I have never heard music sweeter than your voice and although I feel pity for this princess, yet your story is pleasant to hear. Of a certainty I will go to the palace, and try whether I cannot kill this Fomor, and free the lady."

So we came to land, and as we drew nigh to the palace the lovely princess met us and bade us welcome. She led us in and placed us on chairs of gold. After which choice food was placed before us, and drinking horns filled with mead, and golden goblets of sweet wine.

When we had eaten and drunk, the mild princess told us her story, while tears streamed from her soft blue eyes. She ended by saying: "I shall never return to my own country and to my father's house, so long as this great and cruel giant is alive."

When I heard her sad voice, and saw her tears falling, I was moved with pity. Telling her to cease from her grief, I gave her my hand as a pledge that I would meet the giant, and either slay him or fall myself in her defence.

While we were speaking, we saw the giant coming towards the palace, large of body and ugly and hateful in appearance, carrying a load of deerskins on his back and holding a great iron club in his hand. He threw down his load when he saw us, turned a surly look on the princess, and, without greeting us, or showing the least mark of courtesy, he forthwith challenged me to battle in a loud, rough voice.

It was not my wont to be dismayed by a call to battle, or to be terrified at the sight of an enemy, and I went forth at once without the least fear in my heart. But though I had fought many battles in Erin against wild boars and enchanters and foreign invaders, never before did I find it so hard to preserve my life. We fought for three days and three nights without food or drink or sleep, for the giant did not give me a moment for rest and neither did I give him. At length, when I looked at the two princesses weeping in great fear, and when I called to mind my father's deeds in battle, the fury of my valour arose. With a sudden onset I felled the giant to the earth and instantly, before he could recover himself, I cut off his head.

When the maidens saw the monster lying on the ground dead, they uttered three cries of joy and they came to me and led me into the palace. For I was indeed bruised all over, and covered with gory wounds, and a sudden dizziness of brain and feebleness of body seized me. But the daughter of the King of the Land of Life applied precious balsam and healing herbs to my wounds and in a short time I was healed, and my cheerfulness of mind returned.

Then I buried the giant in a deep and wide grave and I raised a great cairn over him, and placed on it a stone with his name graved in ogham.

We rested that night, and at dawn of next morning Niamh said to me that it was time for us to resume our journey to Tir na nOg. So we took our leave of the daughter of the King of the Land of Life; and though her heart was joyful after her release, she wept at our departure, and we were not less sorry at parting from her. When we had mounted the white steed, he galloped towards the strand. As soon as his hooves touched the wave, he shook himself and neighed three times. We plunged forward over the clear, green sea with the speed of a March wind on a hillside. Soon we saw nothing but billows tumbling before us and billows tumbling behind us. We saw again the fawn chased by the white hound with red ears, and the maiden with the golden apple passed swiftly by, followed by the young warrior in yellow silk on his white steed. And again we passed many strange islands and cities and white palaces.

The sky darkened, so that the sun was hidden from our view. A storm arose, and the sea was lighted up with constant flashes. But though the wind blew from every point of the heavens, and the waves rose up and roared around us, the white steed kept his course straight on, moving as calmly and swiftly as before, through the foam and blinding spray, without being delayed or disturbed in the least, and without turning either to the right or to the left.

At length the storm abated, and after a time the sun again shone brightly. When I looked up, I saw a country near at hand, all green and full of flowers, with beautiful smooth plains, blue hills, and bright lakes and waterfalls. Not far from the shore stood a palace of surpassing beauty and splendour. It was covered all over with gems of every colour—blue, green, crimson, and yellow. On each side were *grianáns* shining with precious stones, built by artists the most skilful that could be found.

I asked Niamh the name of that delightful country, and she replied: "This is my native country, Tir na nOg. And there is nothing I have promised you that you will not find in it."

As soon as we reached the shore, we dismounted; and now we saw advancing from the palace a troop of noble-looking warriors, all clad in bright garments, who came forward to meet and welcome us. Following these we saw a stately glittering host, with the King at their head wearing a robe of bright yellow satin covered with gems, and a crown that sparkled with gold and diamonds. The Queen came after, attended by a hundred lovely maidens; and as they advanced towards us, it seemed to me that this King and Queen exceeded all the kings and queens of the world in beauty and gracefulness and majesty.

After they had kissed their daughter, the King took my hand, and said aloud in the hearing of the host: "This is Oisin, who is to be the husband of Niamh of the Golden Hair. We give you a hundred thousand welcomes, brave Oisin. You will be forever young in this land. All kinds of delights and innocent pleasures are awaiting you, and my daughter, the gentle, golden-haired Niamh, shall be your wife, for I am King of Tir na nOg."

I gave thanks to the King, and I bowed low to the Queen; after which we went into the palace, where we found a banquet prepared. The feasting and rejoicing lasted for ten days, and on the last day I was wedded to the gentle Niamh of the Golden Hair.

I lived in the Land of Youth for more than three hundred years, but it appeared to me that only three years had passed since the day I parted from my friends. At the end of that time, I began to have a longing desire to see my father, Finn, and all my old friends, and I asked leave of Niamh and of the King to visit Erin.

The King gave permission, and Niamh said: "I will give consent, though I feel sorrow in my heart, for I fear much you will never return to me."

I replied that I would surely return, and that she need not feel any doubt or dread, for that the white steed knew the way and would bring me back in safety. Then she addressed me in these words which seemed very strange to me.

"I will not refuse this request, though your journey afflicts me with great grief and fear. Erin is not now as it was when you left it. The great King Finn and his Fena are all gone. You will find, instead of them, a holy father and hosts of priests and saints. Now, think well on what I say to you, and keep my words in your mind. If once you alight from the white steed, you will never come back to me. Again I warn you, if you place your feet on the green sod in Erin, you will never return to this lovely land. A third time, O Oisin, my beloved husband, a third time I say to you, if you alight from the white steed, you will never see me again."

I promised that I would faithfully attend to her words, and that I would not alight from the white steed. Then, as I looked into her gentle face and marked her grief, my heart was weighed down with sadness, and my tears flowed plentifully. But even so, my mind was bent on coming back to Erin.

When I had mounted the white steed, he galloped straight towards the shore. We moved as swiftly as before over the clear sea. The wind overtook the waves and we overtook the wind, so that we straightway left the Land of Youth behind. We passed by many islands and cities, till at length we landed on the green shores of Erin.

As I travelled on through the country, I looked closely around me, but I scarcely knew the old places, for everything seemed strangely altered. I saw no sign of Finn, and his host, and I began to dread that Niamh's saying was coming true. At length, I espied at a distance a company of little men and women, all mounted on horses as small as themselves; and when I came near, they greeted me kindly and courteously. They looked at me with wonder and curiosity, and they marvelled much at my great size, and at the beauty and majesty of my person.

I asked them about Finn and the Fena—whether they were still living, or if any sudden disaster had swept them away. And one replied: "We have heard of the hero Finn, who ruled the Fena in times of old, and who never had an equal for bravery and wisdom. The poets of Gael have written many books concerning his deeds and the deeds of the Fena, which we cannot now relate, but they are gone long since, for they lived many ages ago. We have heard also, and we have seen it written in very old books, that Finn had a son named Oisin. Now this Oisin went with a young fairy maiden to Tir na nOg, and his father and friends sorrowed greatly after him, and sought him long; but he was never seen again."

When I heard all this, I was filled with amazement, and my heart grew heavy with sorrow. I silently turned my steed from the wondering people, and set forward straightway for Allen of the mighty deeds, on the broad, green plains of Leinster. It was a miserable journey to me; and though my mind, being full of sadness at all I saw and heard, forecasted further sorrows, I was grieved more than ever when I reached Allen. For there, indeed, I found the hill deserted and lonely, and my father's palace all in ruins and overgrown with grass and weeds.

I turned slowly away, and afterwards fared through the land in every direction in search of my friends. But I met only crowds of little people, all strangers, who gazed at me with wonder, and none knew me. I visited every place throughout the country where I knew the Fena had lived, but I found their houses all like Allen, solitary and in ruins and overgrown with grass and weeds.

At length I came to Glenasmole, where many a time I had hunted in days of old with the Fena, and there I saw a crowd of people in the glen.

As soon as they saw me, one of them came forward and said; "Come to us, thou mighty hero, and help us out of our strait, for thou art a man of vast strength."

I went to them, and found a number of men trying in vain to raise a large, flat stone. It was half-lifted from the ground, but those who were under it were not strong enough either to raise it further or to free themselves from its weight. And they were in great distress, and on the point of being crushed to death.

I thought it a shameful thing that so many men should be unable to lift this stone, which Oscar, if he were alive, would take in his right hand and fling over the heads of the feeble crowd. After I had looked a little while, I stooped forward and seized the flag with one hand, and, putting forth my strength, I flung it seven perches from its place, and relieved the little men. But with the great strain the golden saddle-girth broke, and bounding forward to keep myself from falling, I suddenly came to the ground on my two feet.

The moment the white steed felt himself free, he shook himself and neighed. Then, starting off with the speed of a cloud-shadow on a March day, he left me standing helpless and sorrowful. Instantly a woeful change came over me: the sight of my eyes began to fade, the ruddy beauty of my face fled, I

lost all my strength, and I fell to the earth, a poor, withered old man, blind and wrinkled and feeble.

The white steed was never seen again. I never recovered my sight, my youth, or my strength; and I have lived in this manner, sorrowing without ceasing for my gentle, golden-haired wife, Niamh, and thinking ever of my father, Finn, and of the lost companions of my youth.

THE FATE OF
FRANK M'KENNA

William Carleton

~

 here lived a man named M'Kenna at the hip of one of the mountainous hills which divide the county of Tyrone from that of Monaghan. This M'Kenna had two sons, one of whom was in the habit of tracing hares of a Sunday whenever there happened to be a fall of snow. His father, it seems, had frequently remonstrated with him upon what he considered to be a violation of the Lord's day, as well as for his general neglect of Mass. The young man, however, though otherwise harmless and inoffensive, was in this matter quite insensible to paternal reproof, and continued to trace whenever the avocations of labour would allow him. It so happened that upon a Christmas morning, I think in the year 1814, there was a deep fall of snow, and young M'Kenna, instead of going to Mass, got down his clock-stick—which is a staff much thicker and heavier at one end than the other—and prepared to set out on his favourite amusement. His father seeing this, reproved him seriously, and insisted that he should attend prayers. His enthusiasm for the sport, however, was stronger than his love of religion, and he refused to be guided by his father's advice. The old man during the altercation got warm; and on finding that the son obstinately scorned his authority, knelt down and prayed that if the boy persisted in following his own will, he might never return from the mountains unless as a corpse. The imprecation, which was certainly as harsh as it was impious and senseless, might have startled many a mind from a purpose that was, to say the least of it, at variance with religion and the respect due to a father. It had no effect upon the son, who is said to have replied, that whether he ever returned or not, he was determined on going; and go accordingly he did. He was not, however, alone, for it appears that three or four of the neighbouring young men accompanied him. Whether their sport was good or otherwise is not to the purpose, neither am I able to say; but the story goes that towards the latter part of the day they started a larger and darker hare than any they had ever seen, and that she kept dodging on before them bit by bit, leading them to suppose that every succeeding cast of the clock-stick would bring her down. It was observed afterwards that she also led them into the recesses of the mountains, and that although they tried to turn her course homewards, they could not succeed in doing so. As evening advanced, the companions of M'Kenna began to feel the folly of pursuing her farther, and to perceive the danger of losing their way in the mountains should night or a snow-storm come upon them. They therefore proposed to give over the chase and return home. But M'Kenna would not hear of it. "If you wish to go home, you may," said he. "As for me, I'll never leave the hills till I have her with me." They begged and entreated of him to desist and return, but all to no purpose: he appeared to be what the Scots call *fey*—that is, to act as if moved by some impulse that leads to death, and from the influence of which a man cannot withdraw himself. At length, on finding him invincibly obstinate, they left him pursuing the hare directly into the heart of the mountains, and returned to their respective homes.

In the meantime one of the most terrible snow-storms ever remembered in that part of the country came on, and the consequence was that the self-willed young man, who had equally trampled on the sanctities of religion and parental authority, was given over for lost. As soon as the tempest became still, the neighbours assembled in a body and proceeded to look for him. The snow, however, had fallen so heavily that not a single mark of a footstep could be seen. Nothing but one wide waste of white undulating hills met the eye wherever it turned, and of M'Kenna no trace whatever was visible or could be found. His father now remembering the unnatural character of his imprecation was nearly distracted; for although the body had not yet been found, still by every one who witnessed the sudden rage of the storm and who knew the mountains, escape or survival was felt to be impossible. Every day for about a week large parties were out among the hill-ranges seeking him, but to no purpose. At length there came a thaw, and his body was found on a snow-wreath, lying in a supine posture within a circle which he had drawn around him with his clock-stick. His prayer-book lay opened upon his mouth, and his hat was pulled down so as to cover it and his face. It is unnecessary to say that the rumour of his death, and of the circumstances under which he left home, created a most extraordinary sensation in the country—a sensation that was the greater in the proportion to the uncertainty occasioned by his not having been found either alive or dead. Some affirmed that he had crossed the mountains and was seen in Monaghan; others, that he had been seen in Clones, in Emyvale, in Five-mile-town; but despite all of these agreeable reports, the melancholy truth was at length made clear by the appearance of the body as just stated.

Now, it so happened that the house nearest the spot where he lay was inhabited by a man named Daly, I think—but of the name I am not certain—who was a herd or care-taker to Dr. Porter, then bishop of Clogher. The situation of this house was the most lonely and desolate-looking that could be imagined. It was at least two miles distant from any human habitation, being surrounded by one wide and dreary waste of dark moor. By this house lay the route of those who had found the corpse, and I believe the door of it was borrowed for the purpose of conveying it home. Be this as it may, the family witnessed the melancholy procession as it passed slowly through the mountains, and when the place and circumstances are all considered, we may admit that to an ignorant and superstitious people, whose minds, even upon ordinary occasions, were strongly affected by such matters, it was a sight calculated to leave behind it a deep, if not a terrible impression. Time soon proved that it did so.

An incident is said to have occurred at the funeral in fine keeping with the wild spirit of the melancholy event. When the procession had advanced to a place called Mullaghtinny, a large dark-coloured hare, which was instantly recognized, by those who had been out with him on the hills, as the identical one that led him to his fate, is said to have crossed the roads about twenty yards or so before the coffin. The story goes that a man struck it on the side with a stone, and that the blow, which would have killed any ordinary hare, not only did it no injury but occasioned a sound to proceed from the body resembling the hollow one emitted by an empty barrel when struck.

In the meantime the interment took place, and the sensation began, like every other, to die away in the natural progress of time, when, behold, a report ran abroad like wild-fire that, to use the language of the people, "Frank M'Kenna was *appearing!*"

One night, about a fortnight after his funeral, the daughter of Daly, the herd, a girl about fourteen, while lying in bed saw what appeared to be the likeness of M'Kenna, who had been lost. She screamed out, and covering her head with the bed-clothes, told her father and mother that Frank M'Kenna was in the house. This alarming intelligence naturally produced great terror; still, Daly, who, notwithstanding his belief in such matters, possessed a good deal of moral courage, was cool enough to rise and examine the house, which consisted of only one apartment. This gave the daughter some courage, who, on finding that her father could not see him, ventured to look out, and she *then* could see nothing of him herself. She very soon fell asleep, and her father attributed what she saw to fear or some accidental combination of shadows proceeding from the furniture, for it was a clear moonlit night. The light of the following day dispelled a great deal of their apprehensions, and comparatively little was thought of it until evening again advanced, when the fears of the daughter began to return. They appeared to be prophetic, for she said when night came that she knew he would appear again; and accordingly at the same hour he did so. This was repeated on several successive nights, until the girl, from the very hardihood of terror, began to become so far familiarised to the spectre as to venture to address it.

"In the name of God!" she asked. "What is troubling you, or why do you appear to me instead of to some of your own family or relations?"

The ghost's answer alone might settle the question involved in the authenticity of its appearance, being, as it was, an account of one of the most ludicrous missions that ever a spirit was dispatched upon.

"I'm not allowed," said he, "to spake to any of my friends, for I parted wid them in anger; but I'm come to tell you that they are quarrellin' about my breeches—a new pair that I got made for Christmas day; an' as I was comin' up to thrace in the mountains, I thought the ould one 'ud do better, an' of coorse I didn't put the ould pair an me. My raison for appearin'," he added, "is, that you may tell my friends that none of them is to wear them—they must be given in charity."

This serious and solemn intimation from the ghost was duly communicated to the family, and it was found that the circumstances were exactly as it had represented them. This, of course, was considered as sufficient proof of the truth of its mission. Their conversations now became not only frequent but quite friendly and familiar. The girl became a favourite with the spectre, and the spectre, on the other hand, soon lost all his terrors in her eyes. He told her that whilst his friends were bearing home his body, the handspikes or poles on which they carried him had cut his back, and *occasioned him great pain!* The cutting of the back also was known to be true, and strengthened, of course, the truth and authenticity of their dialogues. The whole neighbourhood was now in a commotion with this story of the apparition, and persons incited by curiosity began to visit the girl in order to satisfy themselves of the truth of what they had heard. Everything, however, was corroborated, and the child herself, without any symptoms of anxiety or terror, artlessly related her conversations with the spirit. Hitherto their interviews had been all nocturnal, but now that the ghost found his footing made good, he put a hardy face on, and ventured to appear by daylight. The girl also fell into states of syncope, and while the fits lasted, long conversations with him upon the subject of God, the Blessed Virgin, and Heaven, took place between them. Swearing, drunkenness, theft, and every evil propensity of our nature, were declaimed against with a degree of spectral eloquence quite surprising. Common fame had now a topic dear to her heart, and never was a ghost made more of by his friends than she made of him. The whole country was in a tumult, and I well remember the crowds which flocked to the lonely little cabin in the mountains, now the scene of matters so interesting and important. Not a single day passed in which I should think from ten to twenty, thirty, or fifty persons, were not present at these singular interviews. Nothing else was talked of, thought of, and as I can well testify, dreamt of. I would myself have gone to Daly's were it not for a confounded misgiving I had, that perhaps the ghost might take such a fancy of appearing to *me,* as he had taken to cultivate an intimacy with the girl; and it so happens, that when I see the face of an individual nailed down in the coffin—chilling and gloomy operation!—I experience no particular wish to look upon it again.

The spot where the body of M'Kenna was found is now marked by a little heap of stones, which has been collected since the melancholy event of his death. Every person who passes it throws a stone upon the heap; but why this old custom is practised, or what it means, I do not know, unless it be simply to mark the spot as a visible means of preserving the occurrence.

Daly's house, the scene of the supposed apparition, is now a shapeless ruin, which could scarcely be seen were it not for the green spot which once was a garden, and which now shines at a distance like an emerald, but with no agreeable or pleasing associations. It is a spot which no solitary schoolboy will ever visit, nor indeed would the unflinching believer in the popular nonsense of ghosts wish to pass it without a companion. It is, under any circumstances, a gloomy and barren place; but when looked upon in connection with what we have just recited, it is lonely, desolate, and awful.

$\mathcal{S}$OURCES

~

William Carleton, "The Fate of Frank McKenna," from *Fairy and Folk Tales of Ireland* (ed. W. B. Yeats), Pan Books Limited, 1979.

Thomas Crofton Croker, "The Crookened Back" and "The Legend of Knockgrafton," from *Fairy Legends and Traditions of the South of Ireland*, John Murry, 1862: "The Soul Cages," from *Fairy and Folk Tales of Ireland* (ed. W. B. Yeats), Pan Books Limited, 1979.

Lady Gregory, "Sea Stories," from *Vision and Beliefs in the West of Ireland*, Colin Smythe Limited, 1970. Reprinted by permission of Colin Smythe Limited.

Couglas Hyde, "The Student Who Left College" and "Knock Mulruana," from *The Stone of Truth and Other Irish Folk Tales*, Irish Academic Press, 1997: "Teig O'Kane and the Corpse," from *Fairy and Folk Tales of Ireland* (ed. W. B. Yeats), Pan Books limited, 1979. Reprinted by permission of Mr. D. Sealy.

Joseph Jacobs, "The Story of Deirdre," from *Celtic Fairy Tales*, The Bodley Head, 1970; "The Fate of the Children of Lir," from *Great Folktales of Ireland* (ed. Mary McGarry), Frederick Muller, 1979.

Dr. P. W. Joyce, "Oisin in Tir Na nOg" from *Old Celtic Romances*, Nutt, 1894: and "Fergus O'Mara and the Air Demons," from *Fairy and Folk Tales of Ireland* (ed. W. B. Yeats), Pan Books Limited, 1979.

Patrick Kennedy, "The Silkie Wife" and "The Long Spoon," from *Legends of Irish Witches and Fairies*, Mercier Press, 1976; "The Fairy Child," from *Legendary Fictions of the Irish Celts*, Macmillan, 1866.

Sean O'Dubhda, "The Magic Ship," from *Children of the Salmon* (ed. Eileen O'Faolain), Ward River Press, 1984. Reprinted by permission of Poolbeg Press, Dublin.

David Thomson, "The People of the Sea," from *The People of the Sea*, Arena, 1989. Reprinted with permission from Canongate Books Limited, High Street, Edinburgh.

Lady Jane Francesca Sperenza Wilde, "The Evil Eye," The Stolen Bride," "The Bride's Death Song," "A Wolf Story," "The Priest's Soul," and "The Child's Dream," from *Ancient Legends, Mystic Charms and Superstitions of Ireland*, Chatto and Windus, 1925.